Dedication

To Anne Beverley in memory of the 1980s

The Hollywood Collection

By Sheila Claydon

Digital ISBNs
EPUB 978-1-77299-936-5
Kindle 978-1-77299-937-2
WEB/PDF 978-1-77299-938-9

Print ISBN 978-1-77299-939-6
Amazon Print ISBN 978-1-77299-940-2

Books We Love
A quality publisher of genre fiction.
Airdrie Alberta

3rd edition

* * *

The Hollywood Collection

By Sheila Claydon

Digital ISBNs
EPUB 978-1-77299-936-5
Kindle 978-1-77299-937-2
WEB/PDF 978-1-77299-938-9

Print ISBN 978-1-77299-939-6
Amazon Print ISBN 978-1-77299-940-2

A quality publisher of genre fiction.

Airdrie Alberta

3rd edition
Copyright 1985 by Sheila Claydon
Cover art by Michelle Lee

* * *

Chapter One

March 1983

Samantha hung up the phone and turned to Dominic who was adjusting the hem of a black taffeta dress.

"She's given us Jonathan Aiken."

"What?" He almost swallowed a mouthful of pins. "How on earth did you talk her into that?"

"I didn't." Samantha shook her head in disbelief. "Apparently he's been overworking recently, so the editor has given him our assignment as a sort of working holiday."

Dominic finished pinning the dress and straightened up, stretching with relief. "She obviously doesn't realize what hell this fashion show will be then, does she? Our celebrities will eat him up and spit out the pieces with his rejected proofs. Two weeks in a snake pit would be more of a holiday."

"I know that, and you know that," Samantha said, grinning at him. "But I wasn't about to let Liz Rutherford in on the secret.

After all, as fashion editor of *Elite* she's paid to do her homework, while I'm merely an overworked assistant who knows when she's on to a good thing."

"So do I." Dominic rumpled her hair as he passed her desk on his way to the refrigerator. "I don't know what I'd do without you, Sam—or how I managed before you joined me."

"You didn't," she said pointedly, then nodded as he held up a can of lager. "It took me almost six months to sort out the mess you called an office, and even now I can only think about taking a holiday if I'm prepared to work late for weeks afterwards."

"Tactful and gracious as ever," Dominic grinned as he handed her an opened can of lager. "The ideal personal assistant. If you ever want a reference, darling…"

"I don't," she laughed, taking off her glasses and shuffling papers into tidy piles on her desk. "You know this job suits me very well, and, besides, you'd walk all over anyone who didn't stand up to you."

"True." Dominic downed his drink in two swift gulps and wiped the froth from his mouth with the back of his hand. Then, his eyes twinkling, he said, "It's just that I have this recurring fantasy of an assistant being ever so humble and saying 'Yes, Mr. Blair. No, Mr. Blair. Whatever you say, Mr. Blair.'"

"In your dreams," Samantha aimed a screwed-up piece of paper at his head. It hit the

6

man standing in the doorway squarely on the chin.

For a telling moment there was silence, then he spoke.

"Mr. Blair?" He ignored Samantha.

"Yes," Dominic confirmed. "But I'm afraid it's after working hours, Mr.—?"

"Aiken. Jonathan Aiken." He held out his hand. "I realize it's a little late but when I saw your light I took the liberty of coming up."

"I'm so glad you did." Dominic gripped his hand enthusiastically. "As we're shortly going to have to work closely together, the sooner we get to know one another the better."

"Normally I would agree, but I'm flying out to the States on a private visit the day after tomorrow so we don't have much time. I'll meet up with you in Hollywood on May 28th."

"But that's only three days before the show," Dominic protested, pushing his fingers through his hair as he always did when he became agitated. "It won't give us nearly enough time to agree suitable location shots for each of the celebrities who have agreed to model our dresses."

"A hazard of the business, I'm afraid." Looking anything but sorry, Jonathan Aiken gave a slight shrug. "Maybe we can arrange a short briefing meeting tomorrow instead."

"Not possible because I'm off to Italy in the morning to choose materials for next year's

7

Spring Collection." Dominic's hair was becoming more unruly by the minute.

He turned desperately to Samantha. "Will you do it, Sam?"

Mentally juggling her appointments for the following day as well as allowing some additional time to work on the sketches she would need for a presentation, Samantha nodded. "If Mr. Aiken doesn't mind a late appointment, I can see him at five-thirty."

"Five-thirty will be fine." Jonathan Aiken gave her a cool stare and then turned back to Dominic. "I'm sorry about the inconvenience but I'm sure anything I miss tomorrow can be straightened out on location."

Dominic still looked worried as he followed him to the door. "I hope you're right because we don't have time to waste. We're working to a very tight deadline, as I'm sure you know."

Jonathan Aiken merely inclined his head, his grey eyes disinterested as they flicked from Samantha to Dominic and back again. Then the door swung shut behind him.

"Of all the arrogant, conceited, thoughtless…" Samantha was lost for words as she stared at the closed door. "I take back everything I said about being on to a good thing. He's going to be impossible to work with."

* * *

Samantha stayed up until well after midnight collating the necessary sketches and snippets of material, and attaching typewritten suggestions for suitable backgrounds for the photographs. Three days in Florida was nowhere near long enough to choose suitable locations for each of the six celebrities who had agreed to be photographed modelling dresses for the Dominic Blair Hollywood Collection. Wondering how she and Dominic would cope with that amidst the final preparations for the fashion show, she cursed Jonathan Aiken continuously and fluently as she worked.

"You're a doll." Dominic leapt down the stairs from his top floor apartment two-at-a-time and enveloped her in a bear hug when he found her already working at eight thirty the following morning.

"I'm a fool," she snapped, tired from too little sleep and too much concentration. "I should have told Mr. High and Mighty Aiken that it just isn't possible to set up six different locations in three days as well as organize a fashion show."

"You'll find a way." A good night's sleep had restored Dominic's spirits and he was looking forward to his visit to Italy, secure in the knowledge that Samantha always coped.

"Is this the presentation?" He flicked through the heavy folder on her desk with a whistle of admiration. "It's really good, Sam. Nobody could go wrong with this lot,

9

particularly Jonathan Aiken. You do know that fledgling photographers talk of him in hushed tones don't you."

"Probably because he's never stared at them with his gimlet eyes." Samantha pushed her glasses up on top of her head and grinned, her humor restored.

"The result of viewing life through a camera lens, I imagine." Dominic began to search through her desk drawers, tumbling the neatly stacked contents into confusion.

"If you're looking for your airline tickets, they are on your desk, as is your passport," Samantha said as she pushed him aside. "And behave yourself while you're away. I'm far too busy to mop up any more of your conquests when they cry down the phone, so Italian models you can do without."

Grinning at her, Dominic seized his tickets and passport and stuffed them into the pocket of his leather jacket. Then he picked up his luggage and, blowing a kiss in Samantha's direction, clattered down to the street.

She shook her head as the door swung shut behind him. With his broad shoulders and tightly curling brown hair, he looked more like a sportsman than a fashion designer. People were continually surprised when they met him. Only the graceful movements of his fine hands, and his habit of making instant, sharp-eyed appraisals of their clothes gave him away when he greeted clients. Sam often teased him about his good looks, saying they were as essential to his success as his design skills and that without them he wouldn't have nearly as many clients. Unfortunately, the downside of so much charm and his blatant use of an outrageous sex appeal, was the effect it had on some of the models. Samantha had lost count of the number of times she had dispensed paper tissues and sensible advice to girls who thought their hearts were broken.

With a sigh, she turned back to her desk and tidied it for the fourth time that week. It didn't matter how hard she tried, she could never get Dominic to leave it alone.

The rest of the morning passed quickly as she dealt with a succession of suppliers, each one anxious that their products should be featured in the forthcoming Hollywood Collection. She then had a working lunch with the makeup artist who was to accompany them on the trip.

Sally Bowman was a slim redhead with widely spaced green eyes, a worldly air and an undisguised interest in Dominic. She didn't hide her disappointment when Samantha told her he was in Italy.

"He's always going somewhere," she complained. "Don't you get fed up with holding the fort while he jets around the world selling himself."

"It's my job," Samantha said. "And, besides, someone like Dominic needs a steady home base. Now, for goodness' sake, Sally, sit down and relax. I haven't hidden him behind the furniture, nor is he dating anyone, and you can enjoy a whole week of his company when we go to the States."

"Is it that obvious?" Sally grinned as she subsided into a chair.

"Only to Auntie Sam. And if you want to get anywhere with Dominic, you'd better keep it that way for a while. There are only two things he's frightened of, and one of them is a scheming female with designs on his body."

"Which is most women," Sally sighed. "How can I get him to look at me for more than five minutes?"

"By playing hard to get." Samantha pushed back her chair. "Come on, let's go upstairs and talk about it, and if you want to know why I'm being so helpful it's because I'm fed up with clearing up the debris of Dominic's love life. I have to keep a box of tissues permanently on my desk to mop up heartbroken clients and models alike."

"Don't exaggerate." Sally followed her up the stairs frowning as the message struck home.

Samantha smiled as she rustled up a snack lunch of cheese, crackers and dry white wine. Sally and Dominic were ridiculous. They were obviously mad about each other but neither of them was willing to make the first move and, in Dominic's case at least, that was so uncharacteristic that it had to mean something.

The ultimate commitment phobe, he was running away from something that could turn into a serious relationship given time. She wondered when he would finally realize that Sally was worth it.

She was still thinking about Sally and Dominic an hour later when the telephone rang.

"Jonathan Aiken here." The voice at the other end was clipped and to the point. "I'm afraid I can't make our five-thirty meeting."

"So what do you suggest—that I send the ideas to you by telepathy?" Remembering the midnight oil she had burned on his behalf, Samantha was furious.

"Actually I was about to ask you join me for supper later this evening," he said. "I'm not entirely without consideration, just busy."

Without waiting for a reply he gave her the details of a French restaurant in Piccadilly, told her to meet him there at eight, and hung up.

Samantha stared at the telephone in disbelief. Just who did Jonathan Aiken think he was, and how dare he just assume that she was free for the evening. The fact that she was did nothing to restore her temper. Consequently, she was extremely irritable for the rest of the afternoon and left the office promptly at six o'clock, something she had never done before in the four years she had worked with Dominic. Once she was tangled in the rush hour traffic she remembered why, and her temper was even more frayed by the time she let herself into her apartment and kicked off her shoes.

Eating out was the last thing she felt like doing. All she wanted was an early night. She scowled at herself in the mirror as she unfastened her jacket. Her reflection scowled back, narrowing her blue eyes and painting sharp vertical lines either side of her normally smiling mouth. She groaned. Even her hair needed washing, something she had postponed the previous evening, thanks to the extra work she had needed to do for this meeting.

An hour later she viewed herself in the mirror again with a vague sense of dissatisfaction. Her hair fell in thick waves to her shoulders, darker than usual because it was the end of winter, but still a naturally streaked honey blonde that turned heads when she entered a room. The blue silk dress she had chosen was one of Dominic's creations and it did wonders for her eyes as well as flattering her figure. Even her makeup was flawless—one of the benefits of watching artists like Sally at work, but there was still something wrong.

Jonathan Aiken's cool grey eyes had seemed to write her off when they met, as if he merely regarded her as something decorative that Dominic liked to have around, instead the person who singlehandedly managed the Dominic Blair brand. She pushed petulantly at her hair. If she met him looking like this he would never take her seriously.

After several failures, she managed to twist her hair it into a French pleat. Then she added a pair of glasses. The woman who stared back from the mirror looked cool, dignified and not to be trifled with. Satisfied at last, Samantha picked up her presentation folder from the hall table and stepped out into the street.

* * *

Although she didn't live far from the restaurant, a light drizzle had started which misted her glasses and threatened her makeup, so she flagged down a passing taxi. Consequently, she arrived before Jonathan Aiken. Sitting, sipping a drink, she was amused when he didn't recognize her. He stood impatiently in the entrance for a minute or two until she took pity on him and raised her glass in his direction. Then he did a distinct double take and came slowly across to her.

"Miss Brown?" He was still uncertain.

Samantha inclined her head and gave him just the hint of a smile.

He pulled out a chair and sat down opposite her.

"Sorry. I didn't recognize you. You look different. More…"

"Businesslike," Samantha supplied sweetly. That was when he smiled, realizing she was trying to put him down and prepared to take a joke against himself.

15

The effect was devastating. One minute Samantha was in control; the next, her heart felt as if it had flipped right over.

"Shall we order?" He didn't appear to notice anything untoward, merely turned to the waiter and asked for the menu.

No longer feeling hungry, Samantha ignored the starters and chose an omelet and a side salad. Jonathan took longer, which gave her time to study him.

She guessed he was well over six feet tall, and he was slimly built although his shoulders were broad and he looked as if he worked out. She supposed his face wasn't strictly good-looking; his hair was only a medium brown, and his features were fairly ordinary. It was his eyes which commanded attention. They were a pale smoky grey, rimmed with thick black lashes, and they contrasted sharply with his out-of-season tan.

As if sensing her scrutiny, he handed the menu back to the waiter and looked across at her.

Averting her gaze, she reached for the presentation folder lying on the chair beside her.

"Shall I give you a brief résumé now, then you can ask questions while we're eating?"

He nodded silently as she launched into a description of the Hollywood Collection, using the folder more as a shield than an aid as he continued to stare at her. Finally, she stumbled to a halt, uncharacteristically flustered by his silence.

"Do you have any questions so far?" She pushed her glasses more securely onto her nose.

"No questions."

Something in his voice made her look at him more intently and it was then she realized, with a sudden flare of temper, that he hadn't been listening to a word she said. He hadn't even been staring at her, he had been looking through her, his mind on matters far removed from her presentation.

Remembering his earlier disinterest and the broken appointment, to say nothing of the hours she had spent preparing the material for him, something inside Samantha snapped. Jonathan Aiken was a boor, attractive smile or not, and it was about time someone told him so.

She gathered together the loose pages and returned them to the folder. Then she stood up.

"As you obviously aren't remotely interested in this assignment, Mr. Aiken, I won't waste any more of your time. I'll telephone your editor in the morning and ask for a replacement photographer."

He raised startled eyes as she picked up her bag, then, seeing that she meant it, pushed himself up from his chair and grabbed her arm.

"Don't be so childish, Samantha."

"I'm not being childish." Her voice wobbled as she registered the sudden use of her first name. "I'm just not prepared to waste time with someone who can't even pretend to be interested in something I worked on for hours last night. Most photographers would jump at the chance to be involved with the Dominic Blair Hollywood Collection—so why did *Elite* magazine have to give us the only one who isn't."

His fingers tightened. "I heard every word of your presentation. It was very professional."

His eyes were cold as they stared down at her. As cold as ice, she thought with a shiver. But there was something else too, a weariness that made his words an effort. Hadn't the fashion editor said something about him overworking? For a moment she wavered, then she squared her shoulders for a further onslaught. The collection was far too important to her and Dominic to allow sympathy to get the better of her. They needed a good photographer, had been promised one as part of their deal with *Elite*, so the sooner he realized that, the better.

"Perhaps you think being the great Jonathan Aiken absolves you from taking more than a cursory interest in this assignment. I suppose fashion features are beneath you now you are famous for far more important issues, like conservation and the destruction of inner cities?"

"I couldn't put it better myself." His eyes bored into hers. "I don't want this assignment and I did everything I could to get out of I, but

I'm afraid I'm stuck with it, which means you are stuck with me."

She gritted her teeth as his fingers held her arm in a vise. "Not if I can help it. I shall telephone Liz Rutherford at *Elite* first thing tomorrow morning."

"Which will be too late, because I shall already be on my way to the States." He leaned across and took the presentation folder from her. "Besides, you don't need to worry because, as you so kindly reminded me, I'm the great Jonathan Aiken, so I will deliver a professional job whatever my personal feelings."

Something in his tone, a sort of bitterness mixed with contempt, left Samantha's reply unuttered as they glared at one another. Then she saw he was speaking the truth, that although he didn't want the assignment, he was a professional to his fingertips so he would do a good job. As if he sensed her acceptance, the coldness slowly faded from his eyes as he released her.

"Now perhaps we had better eat before they kick us out for creating a public disturbance."

Samantha flushed and sat down again as she noticed several inquisitive faces staring at them while two waiters exchanged worried glances.

They sat in silence while they were being served, and for several moments afterwards. It was only when Samantha lifted a glass of water to her lips that Jonathan spoke again, and this time he sounded anguished.

"Did I do that?" He took her hand and pointed at the row of livid fingerprints on the pale skin of her wrist.

"It doesn't matter. I bruise very easily." She tried to withdraw her hand, aware of an unwelcome warmth spiraling in the pit of her stomach as his fingers massaged her inner wrist. Then, as he continued to hold her hand, she added, "Please let me go, Mr. Aiken, before we create another scene."

He gave her a somber stare as he reluctantly obeyed, but his fingers lingered for a moment, straightening the sleeve of her dress carefully, and his touch sent a shiver down her spine that she couldn't hide.

She blushed and concentrated on her food, wishing she was anywhere but opposite Jonathan Aiken with his penetrating grey eyes. She hadn't responded to a man like this for years, ever since Danny died. She remembered her dead fiancé with a twinge of pain that had grown steadily less over the years.

If he hadn't died in a senseless motorbike accident, she wouldn't be sitting here now. She would be married with children, a replica of her mother, instead of the hard-headed businesswoman she had become. But the days when Danny had hovered between life and death on a life support system, followed by the even greater heartache of his funeral, had made her determined never to lay herself open to such agony again. She had been just twenty when he died, four months before their wedding, and she had never been seriously involved with a man since.

Now, at twenty-eight, she was unrecognizable as the distraught girl Danny had left behind. Even her family accepted her as cool, organized, efficient Sam, with a calculator for a heart and ambition for a bedfellow.

She frowned as she cut into her chicken. Although she had loved him, she rarely thought about Danny anymore; it was only Jonathan Aiken who had made her recall him.

Irritated, she raised her eyes, determined to banish the ghost. He smiled at her. Not the devastating smile that had shaken her earlier, but a softer, crooked twist of the lips that offered a hint of friendliness.

Despite herself, her mouth turned up at the corners, He nodded approvingly.

"Can I assume I'm forgiven?"

She shrugged, trying to sound nonchalant. "I don't really have a choice, do I. We have to work together so an armed truce is the only sensible action."

"An armed truce?" He raised one eyebrow and his comical expression made her laugh despite herself.

"An armed truce is all I'm prepared to offer at the moment. Anything else…" She stopped abruptly as he leaned forward and plucked her glasses from her nose.

"I thought so," he said, holding them up to the light. "You are wearing these for effect, Samantha Brown. These aren't distance glasses. You're not short-sighted. Come on, admit it. You just need them for close work, if you need them at all."

"I need them for eyestrain," she protested as he folded them into his pocket. "Give them back, Mr. Aiken. I can't work without them."

"Not until you call me Jonathan." He returned to his meal with a low chuckle. "Surely an armed truce can stretch to first names."

"Please let me have my glasses, Jonathan." She tried to stay calm even though something about the quality of his gaze unnerved her.

For a moment she thought he was going to refuse to return her, but he merely shrugged, took them out of his pocket and pushed them across the table. She hesitated and then tucked them into her handbag, knowing that any further attempt to wear them would look ridiculous. When she looked at him again, he nodded in silent approval.

She flushed, annoyed he had caught her out. She would never normally have felt the need to hide behind glasses because her Yorkshire upbringing had given her the twin advantages of plain speech and, when necessary, an acid tongue.

"I do it too." Something in Jonathan's voice startled her into looking straight at him. "I hide behind images, Samantha. That's why I behaved so badly when I first saw you. I thought you were the sort of girl who expected photographers to be macho and moody."

"Why?" She was jolted into indignation.

"Because you were all fluffy hair and huge bedroom eyes," he said, refusing to spare her blushes. "You know the type. They come two a penny in the fashion business and photographers are their favorite prey. I've lost count of the number of times one of them has tried to captivate me into supplying a free portfolio for their venture into modeling."

"You have a colossal conceit," she said. "And I don't have fluffy hair or bedroom eyes." She almost choked over his description, and then flushed again as his grin widened.

"Yes, you have." He leaned forward and tugged gently at a loose tendril of hair. "But they're unawakened, the eyes of an innocent— for all your sharp tongue."

"How dare you be so personal." She tried to sound angry but the words blurred to a whisper as his hand slid over her cheek and traced the outline of her mouth.

"I've dared many things in my life, Samantha Brown." He wasn't smiling any longer and the silence lengthened between them as they stared at one another.

A discreet cough from the waiter interrupted them and brought Samantha to her senses. She refused a dessert. All she wanted was to get home, as far away from Jonathan Aiken as possible. Life was quite hectic enough already, without the added complication of overheated emotions.

"Two coffees please, and the cheeseboard." Jonathan also refused a dessert, and by the time he had selected savory crackers and a slice of Stilton, Samantha had regained her poise. As he bit into a biscuit, she reminded him of the reason for their meeting. He gave a wry smile.

"Go right ahead, and I promise I'll listen to every word."

She inclined her head, trying desperately to cling to her business-like image in the hope that it would stop her stomach lurching every time she looked at him, and proceeded to give him a more detailed presentation of what was expected of him.

This time he listened properly, and then asked so many questions that she forgot to be self-conscious as they discussed the fashion show and the celebrity photos. And such was his apparent interest that their meal extended to another cup of coffee and a liqueur before they finished.

Later, as they left the restaurant, he became more withdrawn. Wondering what he was thinking about, she breathed a sigh of relief when he hailed a taxi. She was eager to get home and forget the effect he had had on her earlier. While they were discussing business her stomach had calmed completely so now she was more than ready to pretend it had never happened.

A cruising taxi did a sharp U-turn and swerved to a halt beside them. Samantha opened the door with a relieved smile.

"Good night, Jonathan, and thank you for the meal…" her voice trailed away uncertainly as he put his hands on her shoulders.

"Good night, Samantha Brown. See you in LA." His kiss was gentle, a mere brushing of his lips against her cheek, and then he was gone, striding up Piccadilly without a backward glance.

She didn't remember the taxi ride home, or even much of their conversation, but the imprint of his lips on her flushed skin stayed with her throughout the night, so that she tossed and turned feverishly, angry at her unexpected vulnerability. Angry with Jonathan.

Chapter Two

She was still angry the following morning when Dominic returned from Italy with a suitcase full of samples and a hangover.

"Some aspirins Sam, and strong coffee—gallons and gallons of strong coffee," he groaned as he dropped his bags onto the floor and peeled off his jacket.

"You'll have orange juice and like it," she snapped, taking a carton of juice from the refrigerator and snipping off a corner with her scissors. "And it's about time you stopped burning the candle at both ends Dominic. You need to settle down. You can't carry on like this forever."

He downed half a pint of orange juice in one go and then held out his glass for more. His eyes were pink-rimmed and he desperately needed a shave.

"For goodness' sake go and tidy yourself up before Lady Rogers comes in for her fitting. Then, if you're quick, you can tell me about Italy, sparing me the gory details of whatever you got up to last night, of course."

"Yes, ma'am." He sketched a salute and then groaned and held his head. "Did I ever tell you, you have no heart, Sam?"

"Frequently." She pushed him towards the stairs leading up to his apartment. "Now please hurry or you'll lose one of your wealthiest clients. Even Lady R would draw the line at dealing with someone who appears to have slept in his clothes—and she's one of your greatest fans."

"In every sense of the word." He chuckled as he picked up his bags, and Samantha laughed with him as they visualized the majestic proportions of Lady Rogers. At six feet one inch and twenty stone, dressing her was rather like rigging out a ship in full sail.

"A small cup of coffee?" Dominic wheedled hopefully, taking advantage of her returning good humor.

"All right," she relented. "But only if you promise to hurry."

"You're a love." He dropped a kiss on top of her head and retreated up the stairs.

She followed him five minutes later carrying a pint of milk and a pad full of notes. Dominic's apartment and the office overflowed into each other because of the nature of his work, so despite the chaos of his working habits, his sitting room was always immaculate and ready to receive clients. She filled the jug at the sink and then spooned in freshly ground coffee and left it percolating while she went into

27

Dominic's bedroom. As she had expected, he had unpacked the material samples before he did anything else.

They were spread across his bed in a profusion of pastel greys and blues, mixed with lilac and an occasional deeper mauve. She exclaimed aloud at the textures, from pure silk through a whole range of delicate man-made fabrics for evening dresses and shirts, to crisp pre-creased cottons for day wear. Nothing was too heavy but she could see that the warmth necessary for the worst days of an English summer hadn't been sacrificed.

Dominic, with his unerring eye, was putting the emphasis on femininity and romance for his next Spring Collection, knowing that it would contrast well with the exotic flamboyance of his Hollywood styles.

"You like them?" He finished showering and walked through to the bedroom with a towel wrapped round his waist.

"I think they're lovely." Samantha picked up a swatch of grey silk patterned with lilac. "This is so soft and feminine. All of them will contrast beautifully with your Hollywood Collection."

"You never miss a trick, do you?" He slipped his arm around her shoulders as they looked down at the samples on his bed.

"Nor do you." She laughed up at him. "That's why we get on so well, because we both want the same things out of life."

"You mean money and success." He rubbed his wet head against her cheek, making her squeal with indignation. "But is it enough, Sam? Is this incessant nightlife losing its appeal because I'm tired, or am I just getting old?

She stopped trying to wriggle away from his wet hair and stared up at him, sensing an unexpected wistfulness in his voice despite the jokey melodrama of his question.

She shook her head mockingly. "This is far more serious than a hangover, Dominic."

"As usual, you are probably right Once upon a time a succession of pretty girls and a glamorous nightlife kept me happy but now I'm bored by it all. There's a gap I can't seem to fill whatever I do."

"You need to settle down." She reached up to the towel draped over his shoulder and rubbed at her damp cheek. "You're thirty-three Dominic. You must have sown all your wild oats by now."

"So you think it's time I was put out to grass do you?" Laughing uproariously at his own joke he swung her off her feet, his natural optimism restored. "Good old Sam, you've always got an answer for everything." He kissed her soundly on the mouth—and that was when Jonathan Aiken interrupted them.

"Excuse me." He was retreating from the doorway when they turned towards him. "There was no one in the office so when I heard voices,

I came on up. I didn't realize it was a private residence."

"Jonathan, don't go away." Dominic released Samantha and hurried after him, tucking his towel more securely around his waist. "We use the apartment as an extension to the office. Go on through to the sitting room while I get dressed. Sam is just making some coffee."

"I haven't much time." Jonathan looked tired and drawn despite his tan, and he ignored Samantha.

"Enough for one cup surely?" Dominic was already pulling on a clean shirt. "Besides, I haven't had a chance to ask Sam about your meeting yesterday. Go on, make yourself comfortable. I won't be a moment."

"The sitting room is through there." Samantha didn't like the cool expression in Jonathan's eyes. Wondering why, she suddenly realized he had drawn the wrong conclusion about her relationship with Dominic when he saw them together in the bedroom. It was so funny that she wanted to laugh. She turned hastily towards the kitchen. He followed her and propped himself in the doorway while she busied herself with mugs and spoons.

"I thought you said you were leaving for the States first thing this morning." She tried to break the unnerving silence.

"I was mistaken." His voice was low and tinged with bitterness, and that was when she knew he was referring to something else entirely.

A slow anger began to simmer inside her. She raised her chin, her eyes challenging. "We all make mistakes," she said. "Which is why it's important to get your facts straight"

"I thought I had." In one swift movement he crossed the tiny kitchen, clattering the mugs on the worktop.

She knew he was going to kiss her before he even lowered his head. She twisted her face away but he trapped her against the sink, holding her steady with one hand while the other jerked at her chin, making her look at him.

"Don't you dare." She tried to push at his chest but he was too close, his body touching hers at every point. She began to tremble uncontrollably.

"I told you last night that I've dared many things in my life, Samantha Brown." His voice slurred as he lowered his head, and when she saw the cold glitter in his eyes she knew there would be no escape.

His mouth was fierce and demanding, forcing her head back. She closed her eyes, willing herself not to respond and trying to ignore the sudden heavy throbbing of her heart. At first it was easy because her anger fueled her resolve, but when his mouth softened her control began to waver, her lips parted, and the hands that had been trying to push him away began to cling instead, wanting to touch the warm flesh beneath his shirt, wanting him.

He gave a low moan and pulled her closer, one hand warm on her back, the other circling her neck beneath the heavy weight of her hair. His lips and tongue were exploring her mouth, and she was drowning in sensations utterly unlike anything she had experienced before. She gave a soft cry, a mixture of anguish and release, as her slowly awakening body started to respond.

Instantly, Jonathan stopped kissing her. His voice was a hiss of contempt. "So I did get half of my facts right, Samantha. The bedroom eyes are real, just rather more awakened than I anticipated."

It was as if he had slapped her. A peculiar numbness seemed to fill her chest and then spread outwards, until she was deathly cold. She stared up at him in disbelief, noticing tiny green flecks in the grey of his eyes with one part of her mind while the rest of it screamed silently against the injustice of his accusation.

"Nothing to say?" His lip curled as he stepped backwards. "This time I've removed rather more than your glasses, haven't I."

She gripped the worktop so tightly that the skin across her knuckles grew white. Ever since Danny's death she had denied herself anything but the most casual friendship with men. She had fought hard to achieve emotional and financial independence, determined never to lay herself open to heartbreak again. Yet, in only a few hours, Jonathan had not only managed to break down her carefully erected defenses but had trampled all over them, destroying the tiny hidden part of her that still wanted love and commitment.

She closed her eyes against a sudden rush of tears but when she opened them again they were dry and hard. Nobody was going to treat her like that and get away with it, least of all Jonathan Aiken. Her first impression of him had been right after all; he had a colossal ego that needed deflating.

She wiped her hand slowly across her mouth. "It's you who are the fraud, Jonathan. Everything you said last night was for effect, wasn't it? Secretly you like the silly girls you so charmingly deride. You like having your ego flattered. You enjoy the power you have, and because I didn't fawn all over you during our meal together, you decided I needed a little Aiken education. Well, now you know you're wrong."

She saw the anger in his eyes and knew she had struck home, but before she could continue her attack Dominic joined them, looking fresh and suave in tailored slacks and a silk shirt that was open almost to the waist.

"Coffee ready?" He smiled at them, unaware of the tense atmosphere.

Samantha let go of the worktop and moved deliberately across the kitchen towards him. "It is, but as I have managed to answer all of Jonathan's questions, he won't be staying. He has far more important things to do with his precious time."

"She's right." Jonathan moved out into the hallway. "There's nothing else I need here, so I'll be on my way."

"In that case, we'll see you in Los Angeles." From long habit, Dominic slipped his arm round Samantha's shoulders as he spoke. Instead of ignoring him as she usually did, she snuggled up to him, sliding her own arm around his waist and pleating the silk material of his shirt between her fingers.

Both men noticed, but Dominic's face remained resolutely deadpan as Jonathan turned away with a grim expression and a muttered farewell. He didn't say a word until they heard the street door slam, then he released Samantha with a grin.

"What was all that about? You came on a bit strong for someone who thinks my morals are only slightly higher than those of an alley cat."

"Shall we just say Mr. Aiken needed putting in his place." Samantha forced a smile as she poured coffee.

"So he made a pass at my little stepsister did he?" Dominic shook his head, his eyes full of laughter. "Well, you must admit he's got some nerve. Either that or nobody at *Elite* bothered to tell him that hard-headed Samantha Brown is totally off limits.

Then he noticed her expression and stopped laughing. "There's more to it than that, isn't there? What's the matter, did he get through to you?"

She shook her head. "No more than the average overbearing, pigheaded, conceited photographer who won't take no for an answer. Now please change the subject because I need to clear up a few details with you before Lady Rogers arrives."

"Go ahead." He shrugged, realizing she had no intention of explaining herself and knowing better than to try and force the issue. "But just remember I'm around if you ever want to talk about it."

They smiled at one another, remembering the countless scrapes Samantha had rescued him from over the years and wordlessly acknowledging the unlikelihood of their roles being reversed.

Ever since Samantha's widowed mother had answered an advertisement for a live-in housekeeper when Samantha was seven and Dominic was twelve, they had been almost inseparable, even aiding and abetting Dominic's father when he decided to end years as a single parent by proposing to Ellen Brown. After that, they had felt like a real brother and sister, with Samantha's retention of her father's surname the only barrier between them. So it had seemed

35

perfectly natural for them to work together once Dominic decided to start his own fashion house.

Their temperaments and talents merged perfectly. They had both been to art college but while Dominic had consolidated his inspirational flair at one of the big fashion houses, Samantha had opted for a short business course and then entered the world of magazines.

She had worked her way up to assistant fashion editor by the time Dominic finally broke into the big-time by designing and making costumes for a low budget film starring Hollywood's Lilah Mandeville. To everyone's surprise the film had become a smash hit, catapulting Dominic into the world of celebrity stardom. Suddenly Dominic Blair dresses were the 'must haves' of the rich and cossetted and he needed help. When he asked Samantha to join him she took a deep breath and jumped in with both feet. It was something she had never regretted.

At the beginning they had pooled their savings and rented a small office with a basement workroom, and while Dominic gathered together a group of talented seamstresses, Samantha concentrated on finding reliable models and selling ideas to fashion magazines. In this way, the business had benefited from a double injection of enthusiasm, and nowadays they frequently offered magazine editors a complete fashion feature package that required little more than the services of a photographer.

Often working to tight schedules, and with frequently changing staff, the editors needed very little persuasion to take advantage of Samantha's professional expertise, leaving her to choose locations, employ her own freelance staff of hairdressers and makeup artists, and recruit models. She also made the necessary travel arrangements, and in the past had even paid the bill when a fashion shoot was not up to scratch. That was something that never happened nowadays though, because Dominic Blair was a name that sold magazines, so when he announced that six of the dresses in his Hollywood Collection would be modelled by some of the biggest names in Hollywood, the phone never stopped ringing.

Elite had won, mainly because it had the biggest circulation, but also because it was read by many of Dominic Blair's wealthy clients. Samantha's meeting with Liz Rutherford, its fashion editor, had been very successful, and she had felt on top of the world until Jonathan Aiken happened along.

"There is one thing we should think about carefully, Dominic," she said, beginning to scribble on her pad. "And that's the Hollywood locations for the magazine article. If Jonathan isn't going to arrive until four days before the show, then one of us ought to fly out early and do some scouting around for suitable backgrounds."

"That's your job, love. I don't have the same sort of eye as you. I can't even decide whether the models would look better sprawled across a rock with waves frothing at their feet, or done up to the nines at the Ritz."

"In that case, I'd better speed up my other arrangements and see if I can book myself into the hotel for a few extra days."

"You don't need to do that," Dominic shook his head. "I meant to tell you Lilah phoned. She wants us both to go and stay with her. Ring her back and say you're coming earlier. It'll give you a chance to talk her into modeling one of our dresses. You know she hasn't agreed yet."

"She's only holding out because she wants to see you at your most persuasive." Samantha gave a mocking laugh and then stood up as she heard a noise downstairs.

"That sounds like Lady Rogers. I'll show her straight up so you can do your gigolo bit in peace without me to distract you."

* * *

The next two weeks were a hard slog of fourteen-hour working days as Samantha and Dominic prepared themselves for their big assignment. It was Samantha's dream child, born out of a conversation with Lilah

38

Mandeville when they first launched the Dominic Blair brand. When he started designing exotic, frivolous dresses in vibrant colors she had remembered it and suggested a special *Hollywood Collection* in addition to his usual spring and autumn lines.

It hadn't taken much persuasion because Lilah, now a star in a continuing soap opera, was always on the lookout for publicity. On one of her infrequent trips to London, the three of them had thrashed out the details, choosing June 1st as a mutually convenient date.

Lilah had agreed to organize the Hollywood end and book Morton's, one of Beverly Hills' most revered eating houses, for an afternoon fashion show. She had done a sterling job, drumming up advance notices in the Los Angeles Times and giving several 'exclusive' interviews to magazines, each featuring her in a Dominic Blair dress.

"Anybody who's anybody will be there," she drawled down the telephone when Samantha called her. "I've made it sound like anyone who doesn't have a Dominic Blair dress is a total loser."

"Lilah, you're such a publicity tart that I'm sure you won't mind if I ask another favor of you. Will you model a Dominic Blair dress for us?"

"If it means photographs then count me in." She could hear the smile in Lilah's voice. "Tell me all about it on Friday, honey. I'll have a car

39

meet you at the airport. It'll be almost like old times, having you and Dominic around again."

"And you're quite sure you don't mind if I arrive a few days early?" Samantha queried. "Because I can easily book into a hotel if it's more convenient."

"Like hell she can." Dominic leaned over her shoulder and shouted down the telephone. "You're costing me a fortune in free dresses as payment for all this publicity, Lilah, so the least you can do is feed my little sister."

A peal of laughter greeted him from the other end of the phone and Samantha handed over the mouthpiece with a smile. Dominic and Lilah were two of a kind, flamboyant, newsworthy, and as hard as nails. They liked one another enormously and had probably had an affair years ago when Dominic first started designing, because even though Lilah would never see forty again, she was still a beautiful and desirable woman who openly enjoyed the company of younger men.

* * *

"An LA smog is all I need," Samantha muttered to herself as the aircraft lost height, sweeping across the Los Angeles basin into the pink mist of a Californian sunset that was only occasionally pierced by a high-rise building.

She had worked non-stop until the very last minute, checking every detail of the itinerary, packing the dresses and accessories, telephoning the support team of make-up artists and hairdressers, and last, but not least, making sure Dominic knew where his tickets and passport were. Barring an unforeseen calamity, she was sure she had remembered everything. Her brain, however, didn't accept that and continued to work overtime, repeating endless lists and suggesting problems that might occur. Consequently, she felt very jaded and irritable as she left the plane and walked across the tarmac to the main airport building, a feeling not enhanced by a long holdup in Customs and Immigration, and no sign of Lilah's chauffeur when she was finally cleared.

She sighed impatiently and shifted her bag to her other hand. Perhaps he was waiting by the flight information desk. She twisted her neck, searching for anyone holding up a sign with her name on it, and walked straight into someone coming in the opposite direction. She put out a hand to save herself as one of her heels skidded sideways, but it was too late. Her ankle tipped over with a sharp jab of pain and as her luggage clattered to the floor she was vaguely aware of somebody's arm holding her steady.

For a moment the pain was so bad that she felt sick and faint. She leaned against whoever was supporting her with her eyes tightly closed. Gradually the pain receded until, left with only a dull ache, Samantha was able to straighten up and place her foot gingerly on the ground.

"I'm sorry," she began. "I wasn't looking where I was going."

"That's an understatement," Jonathan Aiken glared down at her. "It was like being mown down by a steam roller."

"You!" She stared up at him in disbelief. "Of all the millions of people in Los Angeles, I have to bump into you."

"That's possibly because I was the only one looking for you." He gave a grim smile. "Actually, I thought you'd seen me until you looked in the opposite direction, and by then it was too late. We were already set on a collision course."

"If I'd seen you, I would have changed direction entirely," Samantha snapped, rubbing her ankle. Then his words suddenly registered. He had been looking for her—and the only person who knew she was arriving in Los Angeles today was Lilah. She paled slightly.

"How did you know I'd be here?"

"Our hostess told me." Her angry rejoinder had wiped any trace of friendliness from his face, leaving him glaring at her through eyes the color of a November sky. "She asked me to collect you because it's her chauffeur's day off."

"You mean, you're staying with Lilah as well?" Samantha couldn't believe it. She had hoped to combine searching for locations with a certain amount of relaxation after her weeks of overwork, but if she was sharing a house with

Jonathan Aiken she would be as relaxed as a sacrificial lamb at the altar.

"I am indeed." He bent and picked up her bags. "Lilah and I are old friends and when she heard I was working on the Dominic Blair assignment, she insisted I join her house party. She says she has a vested interest in the locations I'm researching."

"But that's why I arrived early." Samantha scowled at him. "You said you couldn't meet us before May 28th, which isn't nearly enough time to set up suitable locations, so I've been working myself to death to gain some extra time this end."

"Perhaps you should have consulted me first."

"How? By carrier pigeon. I don't seem to remember you leaving a forwarding address."

"The magazine could have contacted me." Jonathan shifted her case to his other hand and took her arm. "Besides, I never said I wouldn't search for locations, I just said I was leaving earlier than you and Dominic. I thought that was what our meeting was about, you telling me exactly what sort of locations you wanted so I could search them out before you arrived."

"But…I assumed you meant…you mean I didn't need to… oh, no!" Samantha stopped arguing and bit her lip as they began to walk towards the exit.

"What's the matter?" He glanced down at her, his hand tightening on her arm.

43

"It's my ankle. I must have wrenched it more than I realized."

"Let me see." He dropped her case and bent down, steadying her with one arm as he prodded gently at her foot. She winced as he found a tender spot and was then forced to put her hand on his shoulder to steady herself as she teetered slightly on her stiletto heels.

"It's a bit swollen." He looked up at her with a frown. "Why on earth did you choose to wear such silly shoes to travel halfway across the world?"

"Because I wasn't anticipating walking the whole way," Samantha snapped.

"Well, by the look of your ankle you're not even going to make it to the car park." He stood up and put his arm around her waist, holding her up. "I think I'd better find somewhere for you to sit down while I look for a parking space close to the main entrance."

He nodded across to a cluster of vacant seats. "Can you hop over to those if you lean on me, or would you rather I carried you?"

"I can hop." Samantha spoke through gritted teeth because she was sure he was enjoying her predicament.

"I rather thought you might be able to." He gave a low chuckle. "But perhaps it would be easier without your shoes on, or you might end up with two twisted ankles."

She gave him a scathing look and slipped off her shoes, trying not to wince as her injured

44

foot took her weight. Ignoring her protests, he slipped his arm around her waist again and half carried her to the nearest seat. Waiting until he was sure she was comfortable, he gave a faint smile as he turned away. "I'll try not to be too long but it might take me a while to locate a wheelchair."

"You wouldn't." She spluttered indignantly, but he had gone, striding across the airport building with her case swinging from one hand and her shoes dangling from the other.

She watched him go, noticing that he was almost a head taller than most of the people milling around the flight desks. She registered the width of his shoulders too, and the economy of movement that gave a panther-like grace to his walk. She didn't miss the number of female heads that turned in his direction, either. Angrily, she looked in the other direction. He could turn as many heads as he chose. It was no business of hers. He was probably having an affair with Lilah, if the truth were known. Old friend indeed. She pulled a folded magazine from her tote bag and opened it at random, anything to make her look cool and unflustered when he returned.

She gazed blindly at the print as her mind went back to their first meeting and all the empty days since. Try as she might, she hadn't been able to dismiss him from her mind as easily as she had dismissed him from Dominic's kitchen. Her defenses had proved to be beyond repair, and although she had tried to rebuild them with anger and bitterness, it had been a token effort, with memories of his kisses disturbing her sleep so that she woke every morning heavy-eyed and listless.

She blinked back a sudden rush of tears. How was she going to get through the next week? The memory was bad enough without having to deal with Jonathan in the flesh. Even his hand on her arm had sent a flood of warmth tingling through her.

"Are you okay, Samantha?" She jumped as he spoke to her. His voice was concerned, questioning, as he put out a finger and wiped away a solitary tear from her cheek.

"I'm fine." She jerked her head away as if she had been stung.

"Then why the tears?" He sat down beside her.

"Because my ankle hurts, because I've been traveling for hours and I'm tired, and because I've just discovered I needn't have worked day and night for the past two weeks so I could get here early after all..."

"All right, I get the gist of it," he interrupted her, holding up a protesting hand. "And I'm sorry if there was a misunderstanding about the locations. Maybe I didn't make myself clear."

"An apology from the great Jonathan Aiken." Bitterness goaded Samantha on. "Is that some kind of record?"

His face darkened. "If this is going to degenerate into a slanging match, then it's time I took you back to Lilah's. You're obviously more tired than you realize."

As he spoke he stood up and unfolded a canvas wheelchair that he'd parked behind her seat. Samantha watched him in disbelief.

"If you think you're going to push me across the airport in that, then you're very much mistaken."

"It's that or I'll carry you." His expression didn't change. "Now for goodness' sake, behave yourself—or are we going to have another public scene?"

She glared up at him, ready to fight, but something in his eyes told her she had met her match this time, and that he would do just what he threatened and carry her through the airport if she made a fuss.

Chapter Three

A sleek white Mercedes was parked on double yellow lines outside the entrance. An airport official was guarding it. He smiled when he saw the wheelchair, and opened the passenger door. Ignoring Jonathan's proffered arm, Samantha slid angrily into the car and started to flick through her magazine while he tipped the attendant. Anything to prevent conversation and take her mind off him.

"I should try reading it the right way up if I were you," he told her as he slid behind the steering wheel. "It's usually more interesting."

* * *

It took them some time to reach Lilah's house, which was set in the moneyed oasis of Beverly Hills, and Jonathan didn't attempt further conversation. Instead he leaned forward and pressed a switch on the dashboard, filling the car with music.

Samantha gave up the pretense of reading and sat back in her seat. It was growing dark and the highway glittered with lights as she closed her eyes. When she opened them again, the car had drawn to a halt on a sweeping, semicircular driveway, and Jonathan was getting out.

"Stay there while I open the door and switch on some lights, "he ordered.

He was back in a moment and his smile appeared genuine as he opened the passenger door.

"How's the ankle?"

"Better, I think." Samantha ignored his hand and put her feet to the ground. For a moment she thought her optimism was justified, but as she put her weight on the damaged ankle, a shooting pain made her gasp.

"Stop being so damned obstinate and let me help you." Jonathan slipped his arm round her waist for the third time that day and held her upright. "You can't possibly manage the steps, let alone the several acres of floor between here and your bedroom. Come on Samantha, forgive me for teasing you about reading the magazine upside down, forgive me for being here. Let's go right back to our armed truce. Remember?"

Samantha remembered their truce only too well. That had been when he removed her glasses. It had also been before he made a snap judgment about her relationship with Dominic.

Jonathan saw the expression in her eyes and gave a twisted smile. "I'm sorry about everything if it's any consolation." His face was shadowed by the concealed lighting that illuminated the house. "Can't we go right back and start afresh? Can't we forget London, forget

49

Dominic, and try to be friends? I know we haven't had a very good start but as we're both Lilah's guests, it will be a lot more comfortable for everyone if we try."

"I suppose you're right." Her voice was deliberately cool and disinterested. "A full-scale war would be a bit embarrassing for Lilah."

He didn't answer but merely swung her up into his arms and carried her through Lilah's grand entranceway and then up an elegant marble staircase to a spacious blue and grey guest suite on the second story.

"Thank you." She kept her eyes averted as he lowered her onto the bed. "I can manage now if you'll just tell Lilah I'm here."

"I'm afraid you'll have to make do with me. Lilah is out. It's her chauffeur's day off, and her housekeeper is visiting a sick sister."

Samantha was startled into looking straight at him, and he grinned. "Don't worry. I shan't take advantage of you again. Next time it will be mutual."

"What on earth makes you think there will ever be a next time?" Samantha was playing for time, trying to come to terms with the fact that they were alone in the house, trying to smother the memory of his closeness as he carried her through the house, the warmth of his fingers through the thin cotton of her dress, the heavy beating of his heart against her breast.

50

"This does." His hand was gentle on her neck, the fingers seeking the rapidly beating pulse at her throat.

"We're both adult, Samantha, so it's a waste of time trying to deny it. You knew that when we had dinner together, and you know it now."

"You're insufferable." She snatched at his fingers but he was faster, pinning her hands together as he pulled her up from the bed.

"I probably am. But right now you can't do a thing about it. So be a good girl and get ready for bed while I track down the supper Lilah's housekeeper left for you. After all, I am meant to be looking after you."

"I'm perfectly capable of looking after myself thank you." Samantha tried to twist herself out of his grasp, disturbed by the pressure of his fingers on her arm and the warmth of his breath on her cheek.

"You're not tonight," he corrected, giving her a gentle shake. "You're overtired and your ankle hurts, so stop fighting me and try to be friends. I've apologized for everything I've done in the past to upset you, so the least you can do is to accept my offer of help graciously."

"You don't seem to have left me with any choice." She stopped struggling and looked up at him. "When will Lilah be back?"

"When it suits her," he said, with a wry smile. "You know Lilah—she's a law unto herself."

"Is that why you're such good friends?" Samantha couldn't resist a final jibe. "Birds of a feather, and all that."

"Always determined to have the last word, aren't you? Let's just say that Lilah and I go back a long way, to before she was famous. Now can I safely let go of you or will you start being independent again?"

"It's safe to let go." Samantha gave him a wan smile as his reference to Lilah sank home. It confirmed her suspicion that he was one of her many conquests and that, coupled with a tiring journey and the pain in her ankle, took all the fight out of her. Silly to think she had ever been disturbed by him, had ever read anything into his behavior that suggested he might be interested in her. To him she was just another female who might be available and, just like Dominic, he couldn't resist the challenge. A truce was not going to be so difficult after all.

* * *

By the time Jonathan returned, she had managed to find her nightwear and slip out of her traveling clothes. She had just finished fastening her robe when he tapped on the door.

"Come in." She hopped across to an armchair and sat down.

"Parma ham with avocado salad, followed by fresh pineapple and a glass of dry white wine." Jonathan lowered the tray onto a coffee table and smiled at her.

"It sounds delicious." Samantha eyed the tray appreciatively, then stiffened when she saw two glasses of wine and double stacked plates.

"In view of our new truce, I thought it would be a bit ridiculous to eat in separate rooms." He removed the cover from one of the plates and handed her a beautifully arranged salad.

"Of course." Samantha hoped she sounded more gracious than she felt. It was one thing to dismiss Jonathan as a lady-killer, another to sit through a meal with him in the intimacy of her suite, wearing only a thin silk robe over her nightdress, and with a huge double bed a few steps away in the adjoining bedroom. She pulled her robe more decorously across her knees, and then flushed slightly as he grinned.

"I've already told you I shan't take advantage of you, so relax and tell me where you'd like to go tomorrow."

"Tomorrow?" She frowned.

"In our search for locations." He lowered himself to the floor and reached for his wine.

"I hadn't really thought." She tried to concentrate on her meal. "I don't know Hollywood very well, so I was going to ask Lilah for some suggestions."

"In that case you'd better come with me and see if you approve of my choice." Jonathan tucked into his salad with gusto. "It's quite a

53

while since I was last in LA, but I've had a quick scout round since I arrived and nothing seems to have changed very much except for the Walk of Fame which is a few yards longer than it was on my last visit."

He raised an eyebrow at Samantha's blank expression. "Don't tell me you haven't heard of the Walk of Fame. A celebrity hasn't made it until they've had their hands and feet imprinted in Hollywood Boulevard."

"Has Lilah?" Samantha bit her lip.

"Naturally." Jonathan looked suitably solemn, and in a moment they were both helpless with laughter.

"How many of them are there?" Samantha asked when she paused for breath.

"At least two and a half thousand at last count," Jonathan chuckled. "They're embedded in the sidewalks of Hollywood Boulevard and Vine Street. It's a ritual that will go on and on until they run out of stars or sidewalks, whichever comes first."

"Then it has to be one of our locations." Samantha gave him her first genuine smile. "Do you think Lilah would model a dress for us with that as a background?"

"Not with all that competition engraved in the concrete behind her?" Jonathan shook his head. "Lilah will opt for something far more low key—like the Hollywood Bowl."

"You are absolutely right, darling." Lilah swept into the room on a drift of crimson silk.

"I'm so glad I won't have to waste time explaining my requirements.

"Samantha honey." She kissed the air near Samantha's cheek. "Although Jonathan told me that you two know one another, I didn't realize you were quite such good friends." She raised a quizzical eyebrow, her beautiful brown eyes darting from Samantha's robe to the empty plates.

"We're not." Samantha blushed scarlet. "I twisted my ankle at the airport, and because the stairs were too much for me, Jonathan brought our supper up here."

"You hardly need to make excuses to me, sweetie." Lilah gave her a mocking smile. "This is freedom house—something that Dominic took full advantage of the last time he was over here, I can assure you."

"I'll bet he did." The color had faded from Samantha's cheeks, leaving her paler than usual. Lilah was obviously determined to take Jonathan's presence in her bedroom at its face value; would be scornful, in fact, if Samantha protested too vigorously. And he wasn't saying anything.

She glanced across at him. He was still sprawling on the floor, his empty dishes stacked neatly beside him, but the lopsided smile that had greeted Lilah's accusation had gone and a frown creased his forehead as he stared back at her.

Lilah, looking from Samantha to Jonathan, chose to misinterpret the silence. She gave a throaty chuckle and turned towards the door.

"It's all right, I'm going, darlings. I've a roomful of guests downstairs who are probably plundering my cocktail cabinet. I just came up to ask you to join us but I'll give your excuses—say the journey was tiring, or something. You two enjoy your reunion."

"Lilah!" Samantha half rose from her chair, but it was too late. She had gone, closing the door firmly behind her.

"Don't waste your breath." Jonathan uncoiled himself from the floor and began loading their plates onto the tray. "If Lilah has decided we're in the middle of an affair then all protests will fall on stony ground."

"You didn't exactly say anything to make her think otherwise, did you?" Samantha flushed angrily. "Why didn't you back up my explanation?"

"Because I knew it would be a waste of time." Jonathan moved towards her chair. "In Lilah's eyes, we are already compromised. Besides, I don't really mind."

"Well, I do." Samantha was furious. "It's bad enough that we're forced to stay in the same house, without me being labeled as your..."

"My what, Samantha?" Jonathan grinned at her as he knelt by her chair. "Out here it really doesn't matter, you know. Lilah has built her whole career on rumor and innuendo. And life isn't that much different in London, is it, not in the sort of fashion circles that you move in?"

"But it's not true," Samantha stormed. "There is absolutely nothing between us and nor is there going to be."

"That's something I'm prepared to work at." Jonathan reached for her foot as he spoke and then recoiled sharply as she kicked out at him. He rubbed his arm ruefully.

"I suppose I asked for that, but do you think I could look at your ankle without running the risk of permanent injury? From here it looks far more swollen than it was earlier."

"It's fine." She tucked her foot under her robe with a scowl, but Jonathan just chuckled.

"If that's how you want it, but don't say I didn't warn you. If you're prepared to arrive at breakfast tomorrow without a bandage to back up your denial of our affair, it's up to you."

Although Samantha glared at him angrily she realized he was right, and then she despised herself for caring what Lilah and her friends thought. When he held out his hand, she thrust her leg forward, however. He supported it gently by the heel and pressed his fingers tenderly onto a dark red swelling on the side of her ankle.

"You're going to have a nasty bruise." He moved her toes up and down and then made her rotate her ankle. "I don't think it's anything serious, but I wish I'd thought to treat it earlier."

He lowered her foot gently to the floor and stood up. "I won't be a minute. I always carry a first aid kit because my job requires a lot of clambering about—to say nothing of kicks from disgruntled fashion assistants."

Despite herself, Samantha smiled. She knew she had overreacted to Lilah's assumption that she and Jonathan were a pair, and she felt rather foolish. If the same thing had happened with anyone other than Jonathan, she would have probably shrugged it off with a laugh, too used to Dominic's lifestyle to let it bother her. But the effect that Jonathan had on her made Lilah's suggestions too close for comfort.

"That's better." He gave her a lop-sided smile. "For a minute I thought we were going to have to arrange a third truce."

"You only escaped by a hair's breadth." Samantha tried to look stern. "You said you wouldn't tease me anymore and you've broken your promise."

"When?" Jonathan looked indignant.

"When you said...when I kicked you," Samantha couldn't bring herself to repeat the words that had provoked her.

Jonathan made it clear that she didn't need to as he stared back at her from the doorway, his eyes shadowed by the overhead light. "I remember exactly what I said and I wasn't teasing you, Samantha Brown. I meant every word of it."

Although she was tired from her long journey, and the effect of an eight-hour time change to her body clock, Samantha didn't sleep well. She found the quiet of Beverly Hills more disturbing than the buzz of traffic outside her London apartment, and despite Jonathan's expert bandaging, her foot throbbed. She tossed and turned for most of the night and finally gave up trying to sleep at seven o'clock. She could hear someone moving about and assumed it to be Lilah's housekeeper, knowing from an earlier visit that her hostess rarely rose before ten.

She swung her feet to the floor and stood up very carefully, placing most of her weight on her uninjured foot. After a moment she began to relax. Although it still ached, the bandage had done its work and she could stand without too much discomfort. She tried a few tentative steps and found to her relief that she could walk without too much difficulty.

Thankful that she was no longer immobile, she spent the next ten minutes unpacking the rest of her belongings before limping across to the adjoining bathroom to shower and dress. When she turned on the water, however, she realized that her bandage would make showering difficult so, after a moment's deliberation, she contented herself with a wash at the elaborately equipped vanity unit. Then she pulled on a pair of cotton jeans and a matching turquoise shirt and brushed her hair vigorously before braiding it into a thick plait. Pink lipstick and brown mascara finished her toilette, and she gave a rueful smile at her reflection. She looked incongruous against the opulence of the bathroom which, with its sunken bath and gold tap and shower fittings, looked as if it had been designed with silk negligees and tumbling, wanton hairstyles in mind.

She retrieved her own more practical nightwear from the couch behind the door, took a last look at herself in the full-length mirror, and limped back into the bedroom. Lilah would have to take her as she was. She would dress the part of Dominic Blair in the evening, if necessary, but during the day she was going to forget about fashion. It was a long time since she last had a holiday, so despite the doubtful pleasure of Jonathan's company as they searched for locations, she was determined to wring some relaxation from her extra few days in Los Angeles.

Jonathan! She thrust her nightdress beneath her pillow with unnecessary force. Had he really meant what he said last night, or had it been merely a throwaway remark, the sort of thing Dominic might have said if he was intent on encouraging a reluctant model into the right frame of mind?

She frowned as she pulled a pair of espadrilles from the wardrobe and limped across to the chair. She couldn't make him out. One minute he was cold and aloof, the next seductive and determined, and yet last night had also shown her another side: a streak of humor and an unexpected gentleness that was at odds with his other moods. She wondered which was the real Jonathan Aiken, and why he kept blowing hot and cold with her. Then she remembered his hands as he had bandaged her foot, and felt herself grow warm.

He had returned to her bedroom with a crêpe bandage and proceeded to bind up her foot very professionally but without a word. He hadn't needed to speak because every movement of his fingers held a message as he twisted the bandage securely around her ankle. She grew warm as she remembered the shivers of reaction that tingled through her body as his hands touched her bare leg. When he finished he didn't immediately release her foot but held it in his hand so that the warmth from his fingers penetrated the bandage.

"Does that feel better?" He had raised his head and looked at her.

"I…I think so."

"See if you can stand on it." He had straightened up and offered her his hand.

Once she was upright, he had slipped his arm round her waist yet again, ready to support her, and she was suddenly very conscious of the fact that only the flimsy material of her robe separated them. She had tensed and refused to respond to his smile of encouragement, and he

61

had given a sigh of irritation as he slowly withdrew his hand.

She knew she had been silly, that she ought to have been more grateful for his kindness and concern, but something in his eyes had disturbed her. Despite her years of self-imposed celibacy, she had recognized their message and it frightened her. Danny was the last person she had allowed to get that close to her, and he had been a friend since schooldays, someone she had grown up with, whereas Jonathan… she had turned away abruptly, holding on to the back of the chair.

"I shall be fine now, thank you." Her voice had been sharp. "Don't let me keep you any longer."

She had watched him cross the room and pick up the tray, and then addressed his retreating back, her voice strained and formal.

"Good night, and thank you for meeting me at the airport and…and everything."

"You're welcome." He had used the routine American response as he reached the door, his voice disinterested. Then she was alone, left to toss and turn through an endless night and finally admit that he was at the root of her restlessness.

She finished lacing up her espadrilles with a sigh. They just fitted over her bandage and the rope soles gave her foot some extra support. She wiggled her toes into a more comfortable position and considered her reactions. It was no good denying it. Jonathan Aiken attracted her more than anyone she had ever met, even Danny, and his behavior made it clear that she obviously had a similar effect on him, so why couldn't she just relax and enjoy a holiday romance? After all, Lilah, and consequently everyone else, was going to assume there was something going on between them so why not let it become fact? Why couldn't she live a little, as Dominic was always telling her to.

She contemplated the thought for a moment and then gave a bitter laugh. Whatever had happened to her that she could even consider such a thing? Was she becoming affected by Dominic's restlessness? It was a ridiculous thought. She was quite happy as she was, with ambition more than compensating for a lonely bed. Besides, she didn't even trust Jonathan. He might be attractive but he was moody and arrogant and far too much at ease in Lilah's home to be only a casual friend. True, Lilah appeared to have relinquished all claims on him, but her casual treatment pointed to a past affair, and Samantha was damned if she was going to fill the gap the other woman had left in his life.

He and Lilah could carry on with their easy morals and smutty insinuations. She would control her feelings as she had done ever since Danny died, and Jonathan Aiken, with his lopsided smile and his gentle hands, could go jump in the lake.

Or the swimming pool, to be more precise, she thought as she limped through the doors that opened out onto the terrace a few minutes later.

Jonathan was surging up and down the pool as if his life depended on it, his strokes clean and controlled, his head down, so that he barely disturbed the water.

Myrna, Lilah's housekeeper, greeted Samantha's arrival with a smile as she nodded towards the pool.

"He's been doing that for the last twenty minutes."

"He's welcome. It's far too early for me." Samantha shivered as she acknowledged the housekeeper's greeting with a laugh. "It's lovely to see you again, Myrna. How is your sister? I understand she isn't too well."

"She's on the mend now, thank you." Myrna busied herself with the garden furniture, bringing out cushions from the summer house and piling them beside a wrought iron table. "She broke her arm a few weeks ago, and with three little ones to look after, life's been a bit difficult for her. I've tried to do what I can, of course, and when Jonathan offered to see to you last night I was very grateful because she had a pile of ironing that I'd been promising to do all the week. I hope you found everything you wanted?"

"Everything was fine." Samantha helped her with the cushions. "The salad was delicious, and Jonathan..."

"Carried out your instructions to the letter, including sending her straight to bed." Jonathan had stopped swimming and he hauled himself out of the pool as they carried the last cushions across the terrace.

He smiled at the housekeeper. "Does this mean that we're having breakfast on the terrace, Myrna, because I'm famished."

"It does if you'll arrange the chairs," she answered briskly. "Joe usually sorts out the terrace before he starts on the garden, but he's coming in late today."

"Give me five minutes and I'll carry out the breakfast tray as well." Jonathan picked up a towel from the table and began to dry himself.

Suddenly, Samantha didn't want to be alone with him. It was one thing to say that she would control her feelings, another to do it. The sight of Jonathan dripping with water, his hair plastered close to his head, had her stomach turning cartwheels. He was a lot bigger than she had realized; his extra inches and finely boned face deceiving her into thinking he was thin. She dragged her eyes away from him and tried to hurry after Myrna, but her foot hampered her and the housekeeper disappeared into the house while she was still attempting to cross the terrace.

"Still fighting me, Samantha?" Jonathan rubbed vigorously at his hair and then raked it into shape with his fingers.

"Of course not." She swung round sharply. "I just thought Myrna might appreciate some help."

"You'll have to do better than that," he said with a grin." As you've stayed here before, you know perfectly well that she can't bear anyone in her kitchen when she's cooking. Now come over here and relax while I get changed. This is the best part of the day."

He picked up two cushions as he spoke and arranged them on a lounger at the poolside. Samantha felt a frisson of alarm as she watched him. She hadn't realized quite how perfect his body was. Ignoring him wasn't going to be as easy as she had anticipated, particularly if he kept looking at her like that...

As if he could read her thoughts, his teeth gleamed white against the brown of his face— but he didn't say anything, merely gestured towards the chair. She limped across to it rather self-consciously, avoiding his eyes and, more importantly, the sight of his near nakedness. It made no difference though, because she didn't need to look at him to see the smooth expanse of his chest or the whorls of golden brown hair that patterned a V against his stomach and glistened on his legs.

"Good girl." His hand was feather light against her neck as she dropped onto the lounger, and then he was gone, striding through the house, whistling softly under his breath.

Samantha stared after him, her fingers going unconsciously to her neck. Why had he spoken to her like that? As if she were little more than a child who needed to be cajoled into good behavior?

Unexpected tears prickled her eyelids. It was a long time since anyone had treated her with that kind of gentleness. Dominic, although affectionate, was boisterous and extrovert; her mother and stepfather lived in North Yorkshire, too far away for more than fleeting visits at Christmas and Easter; and she had actively discouraged anyone else from physical contact, so Jonathan's fingers against her neck and the softness in his voice were a startling experience.

Angrily, she shook herself and blinked back her tears. She must be more tired than she had realized to let such a little thing upset her. When she returned to London she would insist that both she and Dominic have a proper holiday, a chance to recharge their batteries. She would take a pile of books and soak up the sun for a fortnight, three weeks even.

She was still making plans when Jonathan returned and began to set the chairs round the table and slip the cushions into place.

"How's the foot? I forgot to ask just now."

"Much better, thank you." Despite herself, Samantha smiled at him, responding to the friendliness in his voice.

"Good, because we've a busy itinerary today." He pushed the last chair into place just as Myrna appeared with a laden tray.

"Hey, I thought I was supposed to be doing that." He hurried across and took it from her.

"It's no trouble, but I'd be glad if you would return it to the kitchen when you've finished." She turned back towards the house with a smile of thanks. "Lilah is giving a dinner party this evening so I shall have my hands full all day."

Samantha was amused by the deftness with which Jonathan unloaded the tray. He was certainly a man of many moods and abilities.

"What's so funny?" He poured her a glass of orange juice.

"You are." She accepted it gratefully. "In the space of about ten minutes you've switched from macho man, plowing up and down the pool as if a shark were after you, to a fair imitation of Myrna herself!"

"You're obviously on the mend," he said, pulling a face. "Your sharp edges are showing."

"I meant it as a compliment." Samantha reached for the fruit bowl.

"You mean a tribute to modern man who has learned how to keep fit while coping with the long list of domestic chores that working women have chosen to pile upon him?"

"Something like that," Samantha agreed as she bit into a peach, and then dabbed hurriedly at her face as the juice began to trickle down her chin.

"Put it all down to my single state." He gave a comical sigh as he piled waffles and eggs onto his plate. "I've had to learn to be everything to the opposite sex. You know, a sort of caveman cook."

"Or a last-ditch Lothario!" Samantha giggled as he gave her a cold look.

"I meant no such thing." His voice was stern although his eyes twinkled. "And for that you will eat an entire meal cooked by me while you are here, as proof of my diverse talents."

"Is that a threat or a promise?" Samantha was finding it surprisingly easy to fall into a teasing repartee, as if the touch of his fingers on her neck had released another softer girl. Or perhaps it was the holiday atmosphere, with breakfast on the terrace and casual clothes, not having to worry about the Dominic Blair image. Before he had time to answer her, however, Lilah joined them.

She drifted through the French doors in a lacy negligee, her face half-covered by enormous sunglasses. She eyed Jonathan's breakfast with distaste.

"Do you have to behave in such a disgustingly healthy manner, Jon? First you wake me up with your early morning dip, and then I'm forced to watch you consume a vast quantity of food at a time when all sensible mortals can just about manage coffee."

69

"You ought to try it." Jonathan grinned up at her as he mopped up some egg yolk with a forkful of waffle. "It would help you to greet each day with enthusiasm."

"Nothing could do that." Lilah gave an exaggerated shudder as she made her way across to the lounger that Samantha had vacated. "Bring me a cup of coffee, darling, and a small glass of fruit juice."

"So it was a heavy session last night, was it?" Jonathan winked at Samantha as he poured some coffee.

"I just want to be left to die in peace." Lilah arranged herself on the lounger and accepted the coffee gratefully.

"As Samantha and I are about to embark on a tour of Hollywood, that can easily be arranged," Jonathan said cheerfully as he began to stack up the breakfast dishes. "We shan't disturb you again until this evening."

"You'll be back in time for my dinner party though, won't you?" Lilah swiveled slightly so that she could include Samantha in the conversation. "I've invited everyone who has agreed to model your collection."

"Lilah, you're marvelous," Samantha left her chair and perched on the end of the lounger. "It'll give me a chance to brief them, so that by the time Dominic arrives with the dresses they'll know what's expected of them."

"You mean be professional, work hard, and do it all for the sake of a free Dominic Blair dress and a whole lot of publicity." Lilah gave an unbecoming cackle of laughter. "I hope Dominic appreciates what a treasure he has in you, Samantha. You'd wring blood from a stone for that company of his."

She turned back to Jonathan with a smile. "Do you realize that this child has single-handedly masterminded Dominic Blair into one of the foremost positions in the fashion world. Somehow she has even persuaded Hollywood stars with a capital S to model his dresses free of charge."

"I think Dominic's designs have quite a lot to do with it too." Samantha gave a light laugh, embarrassed by Lilah's over-the-top enthusiasm. "Without him I wouldn't have anything to mastermind."

"And I suppose he's still the same as ever." Lilah drained her coffee cup. "Hitting the high spots with a string of beauties while you stay at home and clear up the chaos?"

"Something like that," Samantha laughed. "But he works hard too, Lilah. He's been working day and night on this Hollywood Collection. It's really terrific."

"In that case, go and find a suitable location for my photograph." Lilah adjusted her negligee and settled back on the lounger. "All this early morning discussion has worn me out so go away so I can have a couple of hours sleep undisturbed."

71

Still laughing, Samantha pushed herself up from the lounger and turned to Jonathan. "Let me help you with the breakfast tray," she began, and then stopped when she saw the expression on his face.

It was cold and distant again, and yet there was something indefinable in his eyes, a mixture of pity and contempt—and was it anger? She stared back at him, the smile slowly fading from her face. His lighthearted charm had gone, leaving him hard-faced and withdrawn. She was reminded of their first meeting until Lilah's remarks sank home.

Of course! He still thought she was Dominic's girlfriend so was reacting to Lilah's description of their lifestyle. A half smile tugged at the corner of her mouth as she contemplated setting the matter straight. It would serve him right if he felt ridiculous, pay him back for jumping to conclusions. It would be just desserts for his overbearing attitude and his general pushiness towards her.

She opened her mouth to explain the situation, ready to join Lilah in laughter, but it was too late. Jonathan had finished stacking the breakfast tray and was on his way indoors.

"I'll have the car by the front door in five minutes," he rapped out over his shoulder. "Don't be longer than you have to be because we've a lot to fit in today."

His tone suggested he thought she was in the habit of being late and keeping people

72

waiting, and she knew she had once more been relegated to the level of a decorative accessory to Dominic's thriving fashion house, someone likely to be overconcerned with her looks and not prepared to leave the safety of Lilah's high-walled garden without an hour's posturing and painting before the mirror.

She flushed angrily, a sharp retort on her tongue, but he had gone. When she turned back to the terrace, Lilah appeared to be asleep and unaware of the sudden tension between them.

With a heavy frown she limped back into the house and collected her leather tote bag, a pencil and notepad. Then, pausing only to brush her teeth and refusing even to renew her lipstick in the light of Jonathan's pointed remark, she made her way to the front drive.

To her immense satisfaction, he was nowhere to be seen, and she perched herself ostentatiously on the steps to wait for him. After a moment or two, however, she began to see the funny side of the situation. Here she was, trying desperately to prove something to a man she found attractive and boorish by turns, when less than an hour earlier she had sworn to control her feelings and keep him at arm's length. It was ridiculous, particularly when he had just handed her a very effective means of keeping them apart. As long as he thought she was involved with Dominic he would leave her alone—and that, after all, was exactly what she wanted.

She was still thinking about this when Lilah's white Mercedes swept around the side of the house with Jonathan at the wheel. He leaned across and opened the passenger door when he saw her, a pair of sunglasses hiding his expression. For a moment she was tempted to ask what had taken him so long, but she bit her lip. Keeping him at arm's length was one thing, aggravating his erratic temper was entirely another.

She slid into the car without a word and tossed her bag onto the rear seat beside his camera. He waited for her to close the door and then released the handbrake and took the last few yards of the driveway too fast before turning east into Sunset Boulevard and the general direction of Hollywood.

Chapter Four

They traveled in silence, past other houses even grander than Lilah's, each with at least one obligatory Mercedes or Rolls Royce in the driveway, and caught an occasional glimpse of gardeners already at work in gardens so perfect that they might have been illustrations in a gardening catalogue.

Samantha gave an inward smile, saluting the money that was the basis of Dominic Blair's future. Without the support of the wealthy and beautiful women who lived in Beverly Hills and shopped in places like Rodeo Drive, women who would pay hundreds of dollars for a silk scarf without flinching, she and Dominic wouldn't be able to achieve their ultimate ambition, which was to cater for the mass market.

It was a side of their ambition that they had hidden from the fashion world, content to multiply their assets quietly until they could expand into mass production. To both of them it was the only challenge, the inevitable outcome of years of hard work. Although they would always enjoy catering to the rich and famous because the money they were prepared to spend brought top quality materials and a freedom to experiment, they had every intention of reaching a wider market one day. In fact, they already had plans to market a limited number of dress patterns immediately after their next collection, patterns that would make the exclusivity of Dominic Blair a little more accessible to the home dressmaker.

Intent upon her thoughts of the future, Samantha didn't notice the changing scenery until the car was slowed by a traffic control under the shadow of a huge billboard advertising a package weekend in Las Vegas. As the car speeded up again she began to concentrate on their route, trying to recall from her previous visit the general direction of Jonathan's journey. Nothing would induce her to break the silence that had settled between them, however, so she contented herself with guessing.

Ahead of them she could see the eye-catching Hollywood Sign overhanging the city from the side of Mount Lee. It dominated the landscape more than the Hollywood Hills themselves, while closer at hand, in the row of garish nightclubs that each wore an air of morning-after lethargy, she recognized the brief length of Sunset Strip. Then they were into Hollywood proper and cruising slowly down the boulevard to the nearest parking lot. It only took

Jonathan a few moments to find a space and maneuver the car into position. As he turned off the engine, Samantha reached for the door handle. Driving in silence down the freeway was one thing but to sit for longer than necessary in the close confines of the car, in a shadowed and almost deserted car lot, was quite another. She wanted people, the glitter of Hollywood, the steadily moving traffic, anything but to be alone with Jonathan and the uncomfortable silence between them.

Before she could open the door, however, he spoke matter-of-factly. "I thought we'd take in Mann's and the Walk of Fame this morning, and follow it up with a drive downtown to the observation area in City Hall. After that, we'll return to Beverly Hills via the San Fernando Valley and the Hollywood Bowl, and if we've time we could stop off at Rodeo Drive for a while to see if any of the exclusive shops there would make a good background. Okay?"

"Okay," Samantha answered automatically, stung out of her self-imposed silence by his apparent normality. She stole a covert glance at him, wondering if he had really forgotten his earlier ill humor on the terrace, but he had already opened his door and was halfway out of the car. The broad expanse of his back told her nothing.

She sighed as she reached for her bag. Maybe her imagination was working overtime, shaken out of its torpor by the extraordinary attraction this man held for her. Possibly his terseness had been no more than a change of gear as he slipped from early morning friendliness to the work in hand. Anyway, why should she care? Attractive or not, she had decided not to let him into her life. And, as he obviously had a history with Lilah, he had no right to pass any opinion about her relationship with Dominic, real or imagined.

She opened the car door irritably, annoyed with Jonathan for his moodiness, angry at herself for reacting so personally, and found herself being helped from the luxurious interior by a strong brown arm.

"Is your ankle going to be all right?" Jonathan asked. He had removed his sunglasses and his eyes were dark in the gloom of the covered car lot.

"It'll be fine." Samantha tried to move away from him but his grip on her arm tightened as he slammed the door shut.

"Well, at least let me help you."

"I said I can manage."

He ignored her, pulling her arm through his so that they walked up the ramp like an old married couple. Unwilling to create a disturbance, Samantha was forced to put up with his support. He didn't speak again but merely matched his footsteps to hers as they strolled along Hollywood Boulevard until they reached Mann's Chinese Theatre.

Samantha stared up at the famous building with interest. Her one other brief trip to Los Angeles in the early days of Dominic's association with Lilah hadn't given her much time to take in the sights, and she was interested in the razzmatazz that had made Hollywood what it was in its heyday.

The theatre was built in three sections with pillars and elaborately carved designs. The central section had a steep-pitched roof, and beneath it columns and bright canopies glistened in the early morning sunshine.

"It's incredible." She forgot her indignation as she studied the theatre with its twin entrances, each displaying identical posters of the latest attraction beneath elaborately lacquered, multicolored lettering.

"It's one of the most visited sights in Hollywood." Jonathan released her arm. "It was built by a showman called Sid Grauman who actually imported those pillars from an oriental temple."

He viewed the theatre through the lens of his camera as he spoke and Samantha watched him with interest, noticing how he slowly panned the whole building as he searched for the best shot. Finally he lowered the camera and smiled at her.

"Why don't you go into the forecourt and view the handprints and footprints of the famous while I take a few pictures? It makes interesting reading."

Surprised into giving him an answering smile, she nodded and limped away from him to gaze at the galaxy of stars whose names decorated the cement in the forecourt. She was still smiling when he rejoined her some time later beside the imprint of Betty Grable's foot.

He grinned and then led her to where Gene Autry's horse had left a hoof mark,

They laughed together, enjoying the absurdity, and by the time he directed her towards the Walk of Fame farther down the Boulevard, Samantha had almost forgotten her earlier anger.

They strolled slowly across the pink terrazzo squares, reading aloud the names encased in the five-pointed bronze stars, until they reached the corner of Hollywood Boulevard and Vine Street.

"Enough?" Jonathan grinned down at her, his hand firm beneath her elbow.

"Enough," she agreed, giggling as she leaned against a wall of the Hollywood Palace Theatre that faced into both streets. "I didn't believe you when you told me about this, you know, or at least I thought you were probably exaggerating. If it goes on for a few more years it will turn into a pink and bronze version of the Milky Way."

Jonathan's smile of appreciation was wide as he lifted his camera and panned back along the boulevard, retracing their footsteps with his lens.

"I think I'll take some long shots of the boulevard, and then some closer views of this corner because it's meant to be one of the most famous corners in Hollywood. Legend has it that every film star has walked across it at one time or other. If I achieve the shots I want, then I might be able to superimpose your celebrities onto my pictures. It will save a great deal of hassle and expense."

"Can you really do that?" Samantha was interested as she recalled the trick photography she had seen while working as a magazine fashion editor.

"Probably. Anything is preferable to traipsing around LA with a bevy of prima donnas who want to be seen and heard."

"Isn't that a bit unkind?" Samantha heard the sharpness in her voice with surprise. After all, he was only repeating things she sometimes thought herself—but there was a slight difference. While she could understand that celebrities needed to be seen and heard, in the same way that Dominic needed publicity if their company was to survive and prosper, Jonathan's tone suggested something else: a contempt and impatience for the people he dealt with that boded ill for their photographic sessions.

"Maybe." He shrugged, lowering his camera. "But I've photographed too many celebrities to have many illusions. Some, like Lilah, can be forgiven for their pushiness because of their generosity and concern for those about them, but others don't always that excuse."

"So you think pushiness is a characteristic reserved exclusively for the famous do you?" Samantha asked drily. "Surely a cross-section of any city, any group of people, will give you the same sort of mix—the generous, the shy, the pushy, the selfish."

"You're right, of course." Jonathan gave her a wry smile. "I'm afraid I've grown bitter in this business. The years have made me less patient, less inclined to make allowances. Not an altogether desirable trait for a photographer in Hollywood, I admit."

"In that case we will definitely photograph the locations separately so we can keep your contact with our film stars to the barest minimum." Samantha eyed him narrowly. "I'm beginning to understand why you didn't want this assignment."

"I promise I'll try not to let it show too often." He gave a short laugh but she noticed the bitter twist to his mouth as he turned away.

He was busy for some considerable time after that, taking shots of the boulevard from numerous angles, striding away from her, even risking standing in the road itself. Finally he took several close-ups of the pink pavement, and then walked slowly back towards her with the camera still at eye level.

"Don't. You're not meant to include me in your shots." Too late, she realized he was snapping her.

"Why not?" His mouth stretched into a grin beneath the camera. "After all, you're a tourist and every tourist has their picture taken at the corner of Hollywood and Vine."

"And in front of the Chinese Theatre?" She gave him a suspicious scowl.

"There too," he agreed. "And maybe at the Hollywood Bowl, Rodeo Drive, Malibu and Bel Air."

"Not if I see you first." Samantha tried to keep her voice stern as he reached her side.

"You won't." He grinned. "Anyway, what have you got against it? Surely you'd like a record of your time in Los Angeles?"

"Maybe..." Samantha shook her head uncertainly as he leaned against the wall, trapping her with his arm. "I'm just not used to featuring in photographs. I'm generally too busy organizing other people's sessions."

"You mean I can claim a scoop? The first photographer to put Miss Samantha Brown on record. Perhaps I could sell them for a great deal of money to one of the less select magazines— you know the kind of article...The Glamorous Miss Samantha Brown of Dominic Blair Letting her Hair Down, or The Jeans-and-Sneaker Side of the Fashion World."

"If I thought anyone would be interested, then I'd be flattered." Samantha found herself smiling up at him. "But I rarely feature in the company publicity. Dominic is our front man."

"A mistake, but then as a mere male I'm hardly likely to appreciate his finer points." Surprisingly, he laughed and then pulled her pigtail.

"Come along, Samantha. You can't visit Hollywood and Vine without sampling an ice cream at the Brown Derby, home of the hot fudge sundae. I'll treat you, because you'll need the energy to climb City Hall."

An hour later, they stepped out of the lift and onto the observation area on the twenty-seventh floor of City Hall. Beneath them Los Angeles sprawled in a tangle of freeways, punctuated by clusters of high-rise buildings and ringed by the San Gabriel Mountains. The Pacific Ocean lapped the huge sweep of the harbor. The view was breathtaking, a colossal urban sprawl that was the heartland of Southern California.

Samantha's eyes were alight with enthusiasm as gazed at it. "This will make the most fantastic background for Dominic Blair's city suits."

"Well, at least we agree on something," Jonathan said. "I thought of this view as soon as I saw your sketches. There is one problem, though; the suits are predominantly grey and blue, and a long-distance shot will give the city an overall blue effect, so I'm going to have to experiment with different colored filters."

"Will that work?"

"It should do, particularly if I use an orange filter for a sunset effect—although if we do choose that one, I'll have to come back again when the sun is lower in the sky."

"Does that really matter?" Samantha was surprised by his attention to detail, particularly in view of his admitted lack of interest in the whole assignment.

"It does to me," he shrugged. "Call it perfectionism, or even fussiness, but I have to know the details are right, even if nobody else cares." His face grew dark. "Sometimes it causes a lot of inconvenience and makes me less than popular."

"Never." Samantha put on her most disbelieving voice and raised a sarcastic eyebrow, panicked into a flippant reaction by a sense of his returning bitterness. It worked and his mood was broken. His smile returned and he tweaked her pigtail again.

"For that, Samantha Brown, I'll take twice as long as necessary while you occupy yourself picking out the points of interest in LA."

She chuckled as he began to busy himself with his camera, and then wandered away from him and stood gazing out at the panoramic view, trying to order her feelings.

The morning with Jonathan had undone all her good intentions. The return of his relaxed friendliness had disarmed her once again so she was finding it increasingly difficult to remember her earlier indignation. Their brief stop at the Brown Derby, to eat a hot fudge sundae and stare at the autographed caricatures of film stars that decorated the walls, had finally thawed her out. In between mouthfuls, he had kept her laughing with star studded anecdotes until he had glanced at his watch and frowned.

"We'd better hurry or we won't fit everything in today. I was aiming for lunch at the Hollywood Bowl."

"I shan't be able to manage lunch after this"

"You won't have to for some considerable time."

Now, watching him shooting, she felt a frisson of alarm. She had never fooled herself, preferring to face life as it really was, so she couldn't fool herself now. If Jonathan chose to kiss her again, despite her good intentions and the fact that his moodiness disturbed her, she knew she wouldn't put up more than a token resistance. Her only defense against such a situation occurring was her sharp tongue.

She was still staring at him, trying to calm her thoughts, when he lowered his camera. Hurriedly, she looked away and stared out across Los Angeles. But it was too late. He had seen the expression in her eyes.

"Don't fight it too hard, Samantha." His voice was soft in her ear. "Sometimes these things just happen, and nothing you do can alter it."

"I don't know what you're talking about."
She jerked away in a panic, too aware of his
closeness and the warmth of his breath stirring
her hair.

"Then let me remind you." He put his arm
around her shoulders and pulled her so close
that she could feel his heart beating, feel the
hardness of his body through her thin cotton
clothes. Before she had time to react, he had
turned her towards him and tilted her chin
upwards so she was forced to look at him.

His eyes, shaded by their thick fringe of
dark lashes, were too close and suddenly she
didn't want to fight him at all. She had been on
her own for too many years to easily forget how
his earlier kisses had affected her. Oblivious to
the other people jostling onto the observation
platform, she closed her eyes, only to open them
sharply a few moments later when the expected
kiss didn't come.

Jonathan was staring down at her, a half
smile on his face. "You see. It's nature.
Something neither of us can fight."

"Speak for yourself." Samantha flushed
angrily as she tried to pull away from him. She
felt totally humiliated.

"You're so sure of yourself, aren't you? So
sure I will follow the path of all your past
conquests. Well, I'm not another Lilah, and if
you think a kiss in the sunshine in LA has any
deeper meaning, then forget it. Our trip through
Hollywood this morning has been a journey

through fantasyland, the sort of thing that encourages unreality, so don't kid yourself it is anything else."

"I won't." Jonathan stopped her fury with his lips, the words whispered into her mouth as he kissed her. The kiss lasted no more than a few seconds but the movement of his tongue against her teeth and the soft pressure of his fingers through her shirt effectively silenced her, so that when he lifted his head she could only look at him, her face pale with emotion.

"Surely this sort of fantasy isn't so terrible." His mouth was still close to hers. "I want you, and I know you want me, so why not make the most of our week together? Why not join in with the Tinsel town game?"

"And at the end of the week?" Samantha's voice was a whisper as she looked up at him.

"The end of the week can take care of itself." A shadow darkened Jonathan's grey eyes. "Live for today. After all, you don't exactly owe Dominic any loyalty if Lilah's remarks this morning can be believed."

Dominic! Samantha snapped back to reality. Jonathan still thought Dominic was her lover, and because of that he obviously thought she was fair game for a week of sex without commitment, a kind of "sauce for the goose, sauce for the gander" situation that would leave her unscathed at the end of a brief affair.

She stared up at him wordlessly as she felt something inside her shrivel and die. For a brief moment she had almost managed to delude herself into thinking that Jonathan was interested in her, Samantha Brown. She had almost believed that something real existed between them that, given time, would destroy the worst memories of Danny's death and give her the courage to love again. Instead, he was offering her what he would have offered any presentable female in the circumstances: a week of sexual thrills, a bit part in Hollywood's fantasy world.

She pushed him away with all her strength. "I mean nothing to you, do I? I'm just another girl, one of the long line you view through your camera lens. Don't you ever look behind the faces, Jonathan? Ask questions, find out what makes people tick. You've made assumptions about me from the first moment we met without ever once asking me a personal question. All you want is the shell, not the person who lives inside."

Her attack had the desired effect because his arms loosened and then dropped to his sides as he listened to her. Angrily, she hitched her bag back onto her shoulder and turned away from him. Reaction was now setting in, and she could feel tears pricking her eyelids.

"Now, if you've quite finished your little game, perhaps we could get on to the next part of our tour." She kept her voice sharp as she limped away from him towards the lift. Nor did she look at him when he joined her, and she shrugged off his hand when they emerged into the sunshine.

"Samantha, damn you, look at me!" He jerked her round to face him. The movement nearly unbalanced her so that she was forced to clutch at his shirt.

"Will you please let me go." She glared up at him, retaining her self-control with difficulty.

"Not until you've heard me out." He shook her slightly, ignoring a group of interested bystanders. "I'm sorry. Do you hear me? I'm sorry if I got you wrong. I guess Lilah's attitudes are too easily absorbed, along with the permanent sunshine. I thought you wanted the same thing as me—still do think it, in fact. But if you want to pretend that there's nothing between us, and give Dominic a loyalty that he doesn't deserve, that's my loss. I even admire you for it, although I'd like to shake some sense into that pretty head of yours. Now, will you please forgive me—and stop looking at me as if I've committed a murder."

"Maybe you have," she muttered, snatching her arm away from him again. "You think you know everything, Jonathan, but you know nothing, nothing at all. Now can we please speed things up because I'd like some time to rest before Lilah's dinner party this evening."

"Anything you say." His face was suddenly grim. "I forgot your dedication to Dominic Blair. I suppose that's why you put up with his philandering? He must be a valuable property for someone with so much ambition."

"It's none of your business." Samantha flung the words over her shoulder as she marched away from him. Her ankle was beginning to trouble her again but she bit her lip as she disguised her limp as effectively as she could.

Jonathan strode silently beside her, his camera swinging from his neck, and they didn't speak again until they reached the car.

"I'll take the shortest route," he said tersely.

She nodded and then added, "Let's skip lunch, too? Right at this moment, sleep is a lot more inviting."

"What do you do, count dollar signs instead of sheep?" Jonathan's voice was bitter as he unlocked the passenger door and held it open for her. She ignored him, and in minutes they had reversed their direction and were traveling back towards the Hollywood Hills.

After a few minutes' silence Samantha leaned forward and flicked on the radio, filling the car with jazz interspersed with advertisements and local news. It had the desired effect of filling the void between them.

Thank goodness she hadn't told Jonathan the truth about Dominic. It would have removed her only defense and she would never have recognized his kisses as the romantic game they were until it was too late. She would have taken

Jonathan's overtures at face value and laid herself open to heartache again.

It couldn't be worse than it is already, a little voice nagged inside her head, but she ignored it and stared straight ahead, watching the Hollywood Sign grow bigger as they sped along the valley. Then they were pulling into the car park behind the Hollywood Bowl, and the sheer magnificence of the scenery ahead of her absorbed her attention.

The auditorium was carved out of the Hollywood Hills, the stage crouching under a massive white dome flanked by pillars that faced row upon row of seats fanning outwards in a wide arc. The vast amphitheatre was almost as famous as Hollywood itself. The ring of mountains surrounding it had been landscaped into a park full of trees and fountains and the whole effect, with the Hollywood Sign still visible above them, was dramatic beyond belief.

"It's even more impressive when it's full." Jonathan's voice was stiff and measured. "I shall have to photograph it with a full orchestra to get the right background for Lilah."

"Would it be possible to have a long shot of the surrounding hills, with the Hollywood Sign in the background?" Samantha forced herself to answer him civilly.

"Of course." He raised an eyebrow, squinting against the bright sunlight.

"It will make a terrific backdrop for a photo of all our models in one big display. The bright colors of their dresses will contrast with the green of the hills, and it can be enlarged to poster size when we're back in London."

"I can see why you're invaluable to Dominic." Jonathan stared out over the hills, his voice tinged with grudging admiration. "That is a PR shot in a million. It certainly won't be your fault if his dresses don't sell."

Chapter Five

They arrived back at Lilah's beautiful house just after four, Jonathan having made no further mention of stopping off at the exclusive Rodeo Drive shopping area. Samantha left the car with a curt nod to which Jonathan inclined his head in return.

She had crossed the driveway and started to climb the steps when she heard him drive away again. At the sound of the receding engine she gave up her pretense of cool indifference and her shoulders slumped sadly as she reached the porch.

Myrna answered the door, shaking her head reprovingly. "You look completely worn out. Whatever does Jonathan think he's doing, keeping you out all day when you're still trying to adjust to the time change?"

"I'm fine, Myrna." Samantha managed a wan smile. "Or at least I will be if I sleep for a couple of hours."

"Good idea. I'll bring you up a drink in five minutes." Myrna walked with her to the foot of

94

the stairs, her eyes anxious. "Would you like coffee or a glass of orange juice?"

"Neither, thank you." Samantha shook her head. "Honestly, I'd rather just sleep. Remind me when I have to be ready for Lilah's party though."

"Eight for eight thirty, so you've plenty of time." Myrna looked stern. "And don't you dare come down a minute earlier than necessary."

* * *

Once in her bedroom Samantha sank onto the bed and unlaced her espadrilles with a sigh of relief. Her ankle was aching more than she cared to admit, and all she wanted to do was sleep and forget about everything. She kicked off her sandals and then unwound the bandage that was supporting her foot. It left crease marks where the joint was still swollen, and her skin had mottled to a reddish purple. She pulled a face and then lay back on the pillows and closed her eyes.

She lay there for a long time, drifting in and out of consciousness, disturbed by the noises of the house, and too tense from her argument with Jonathan to fall sleep. Finally, with a sigh, she opened her eyes. Someone was splashing about in the pool and she could hear voices, Lilah's silvery tones above the deeper sound of a man. It was probably Jonathan flirting with Lilah now he knew Samantha was off limits.

95

She scowled as she swung her legs to the floor, but when she tried to get up and walk across to the window, her ankle gave way. She fell back onto the bed with a cry of pain. For a moment she felt sick and drops of perspiration pricked her forehead. Once the nausea had passed, she stared down at her foot with dismay. Why did it hurt so much now, when she had managed to walk on it for most of the day? Perhaps the bandage had supported it more than she realized. A bath was probably the best solution. It would ease and relax her and refresh her for the evening.

Cautiously, she raised herself from the bed and hopped across to the bathroom, discarding her clothes while she waited for the tub to fill. Finally, when it was sinfully full, and foaming with Lilah's guest bath oil, she lowered herself into it the water.

It was absolute bliss. She lay back with her eyes closed for some minutes, letting the hot water soak away her tensions and her tiredness. Then she unplaited her hair and reached for the shampoo. By the time she had rinsed her hair squeaky clean with the spray nozzle attached to the side of the bath, she felt more ready to cope with the evening ahead of her.

Maybe Jonathan wouldn't even be there. After all, discussions about the style of dress Dominic had chosen for each celebrity model had nothing to do with him. It would probably bore him to tears…

Someone was shouting at her, but they were a long way away and another noise was muffling the sound of their voice. Was it thunder or, even worse, an earthquake? Samantha tried to clutch at something as the earth shifted beneath her. What had she read about Los Angeles? Something about it sitting on the notorious San Andreas Fault. Only this morning Jonathan had pointed out a notice at City Hall that warned that lifts should not be used in cases of fire or earthquake. This morning. Jonathan. It was his voice calling her.

She struggled back to consciousness as strong arms hauled her out of a warm, enveloping sea.

"Don't you ever do that again," Jonathan was kneeling beside the bath, his white dinner jacket dark with patches of water, his hair flopping forward over his forehead. "You could have drowned yourself. Didn't you hear me banging on the door?"

"I must have fallen asleep." Samantha was bewildered as she gazed up at him, still not fully awake.

"A bath full almost to overflowing doesn't make a good bed." He tightened his grip on her shoulders. "Particularly when Lilah's guests are waiting to go in to dinner."

"Oh no! What is the time?" She sat up abruptly and then blushed scarlet when the bath foam that was protecting her modesty stopped doing its job. Jonathan's eyes widened in appreciation.

"It's too late for you to indulge in any false modesty," he said, grinning as he reached for a towel. "You've about ten minutes to save your face."

"In that case please give Lilah my apologies and say I'll be down as soon as possible." Samantha mustered all the dignity that was possible under the circumstances and then waited, pointedly, for Jonathan to leave the bathroom.

"If you're sure you won't fall asleep again." He stood up and straightened his jacket, laughter dancing in his eyes as he consciously prolonged her embarrassment.

"I'm quite sure." Her voice was cold. He turned away with an exaggerated sigh.

"Foiled again. It's just not my day is it, Samantha?"

"Nor is it likely to be," she snapped at the closing door, and then gave a gasp of pain as she tried to climb out of the bath..

Instantly, he returned. "What's the matter? Have you hurt yourself?"

"It's my ankle." She bit her lip as waves of pain made her feel faint again. "I think I must have overdone it today."

"Oh, hell!" He bent over her with a frown. "I've already had my ears chewed off by Myrna for keeping you out all day. She said you looked worn out when you got back."

"She's a natural worrier." Samantha tried to smile but her mouth twisted with pain, and she couldn't stop violently shivering.

"How long have you been lying there?" Jonathan exclaimed, feeling the water with his fingers. "A wrenched ankle and overtiredness are nothing compared to pneumonia!"

"Now you're being ridiculous." Samantha finally managed a smile. "I'll be perfectly all right if you'll just ask Myrna to come up and help me."

"Myrna be damned." He bent down and scooped her out of the bath before she had time to protest. Instinctively, she clung to him as he helped her balance on one foot while he picked up the towel and enveloped her in what seemed like yards of fluffy cotton.

When they reached the bed in the adjoining room, he lowered her gently onto it and sat down beside her.

"There's no way you are going to be ready in ten minutes." He twisted his fingers in her wet hair with a wry smile. "I'll go down and make your excuses, and tell Lilah you'll join them later. Then I'll come back and bind up your foot again."

"You'd better change your jacket and shirt first." Samantha tried to ignore his fingers in her hair as she nodded towards the wetness that had made his fine lawn shirt cling to his muscular body in a way that left very little to her imagination.

"If I do that I'll lose my credibility. When I offered to check on you, I had to walk through a gauntlet of sniggering innuendo, led by Lilah of course. So the sight of me soaked to the skin because of some amorous bathroom frolic is just what everyone will be expecting."

Although his words were teasing his voice was unexpectedly gentle, as if he was on Samantha's side. It startled her into looking directly at him. He stared back, his eyes questioning. She made a slight movement of vain denial as warmth flooded her body. It was all he needed. With a smothered groan he reached for her, pulling her into his arms so that the towel slipped from her shoulders and only the transparent cloth of his shirt was between them.

He trailed kisses across her cheek to her mouth and then down her arching throat as she began to respond. In between kisses he whispered her name again and again, and it was like a caress as his lips traced a path of fire across her skin. Then he pulled back and looked at her.

"Now you know exactly how I feel about you, and you can't pretend you don't feel the same, not any longer. Although I want you more than I've ever wanted anyone I've ever met

Samantha, it's not just about that. It's about need as well. Although I don't expect you to understand why when I hardly understand myself, I need you in my life."

Need. His words filtered through the misty confusion of Samantha's mind as her body answered his with a will of its own. He needed her. Was that the same as love?

"That's not what you said this afternoon," she said as she watched his brown fingers slide across the paleness of her skin.

"I messed up this afternoon." He tangled his hands in the damp strands of her hair and tilted her head back. "I've done everything wrong since the day I met you because I am jealous. Jealous of the hold Dominic has over you, but guilty too. Guilty because wanting to come between the two of you is something I'm not proud of. If you hadn't kept sending me signals that said you want me as much as I want you, then I might have backed away, especially when I saw you with Dominic that day I came to his apartment. For a few days after that I persuaded myself that you were just toying with me, then I remembered how you looked at me, and how you reacted to my touch, and I realized your reasons for staying with him are a lot more complex. It's not just Dominic is it, it's the fact that you work together? Your whole career is tied up in your relationship with him. That's why I suggested a brief affair, something that's as common in this part of LA as the daily

101

sunshine. I thought you would agree, if only to get back at Dominic. I've heard enough about his reputation from Lilah to know that he will probably have a fling while he's out here, so I hoped you would want to do the same. I couldn't think of any other way to persuade you to take a chance on me."

"And I refused." Samantha stared up at him, noticing a darker ring of color round the pale grey of his eyes, noticing a tiny chip on one of his front teeth, noticing a mole at the corner of his mouth.

"Yes, you refused." His hands slid to her shoulders. "And you were so angry when you refused that I knew I was getting through to you. Most people in the fashion world would have replied to my suggestion with a laugh, or with sarcasm, not with anger."

Suddenly he pulled the thick towel up round her shoulders and held her close. "I was angry, too. Angry that you were willing to deny the attraction between us for the sake of your career. I was sure it wasn't Dominic himself that was holding you back, because if you were totally committed to him you would never have looked at me in the first place. And you did, frequently, and your message was very loud and clear even if you didn't mean it to be. You want me as much as I want you. So when I dropped you off this afternoon, I went for a long drive while I mulled over the accusations you threw at me, and I…"

"Jonathan." Lilah's voice interrupted him from outside the room. "Are you two ever going to join us for dinner, or must we start without you?"

Disturbed in midsentence, Jonathan uttered an oath of frustration and released Samantha.

"I'll explain everything to Lilah and ask if we can join them later," he murmured, and stood up.

"Jonathan, don't forget your shirt," Samantha implored as he opened the door—but she was too late. Lilah was standing in the passageway outside the bedroom. She caught a brief glimpse of Samantha through the half-open door. Then she took in Jonathan's wet jacket and shirt, and his ruffled hair, and gave a shrill peal of laughter.

"Samantha fell asleep in the bath," Jonathan said. "She hasn't had a chance to adjust to the time change yet."

"And like a true prince you woke her with a kiss." Lilah's amusement filtered through the door to Samantha. "I'll ask Myrna to hold dinner for another twenty minutes—and if you're not both ready by then, you won't live this evening down in a hurry. It's a good job my guests are all women of the world." Her voice grew fainter as she turned towards the stairs. "Twenty minutes, both of you, and not a moment longer."

"I'm sorry." Jonathan came back to the bed with a frown. "I seem to have made matters worse as far as Lilah is concerned."

"It doesn't matter." Samantha hugged the towel round her, embarrassed by her nakedness now there was a distance between them.

"It does." He put out a finger and touched her cheek. "But now is the wrong time to discuss it unless we want to ruin your reputation forever." He gave her his heartwarming, lopsided smile, the one he hadn't used nearly enough when he was with her.

"Will you spend the day at Malibu with me tomorrow? You can lie on the beach and rest while I take some photographs, and then we can time to talk properly over lunch. Maybe we can even come up with a solution. One a bit like this."

Samantha drew in her breath sharply as he bent to kiss her bare shoulder. Ten minutes in his arms in the intimacy of her bedroom had destroyed every thought but her need for him. His kisses had reawakened her to pleasures she had long forgotten, while his gentleness and concern told her she had misjudged him. He wasn't playing fast and loose at all. He was serious, and she knew their day in Malibu together would be a step forward in a very important relationship. But before that, she had to tell him he was wrong about Dominic, wrong about the reasons for her anger.

104

"There's something you must know," she began, but he stopped her mouth with another kiss.

"Tomorrow will be soon enough. Our twenty minutes has already dwindled. Tell me what clothes you want, and where they are, and I'll fetch them for you and leave you to dress while I change my shirt."

"But..." Samantha protested as he kissed her again.

"No buts." He straightened up with a smile. "And please cover yourself up if you wish to make it to the dinner table at all."

Suddenly she relaxed, aware of the expression in his eyes and enjoying her power over him. He was right. Tomorrow was soon enough.

* * *

Jonathan returned to her bedroom in less than five minutes, wearing a dry shirt and jacket and with his hair tidied. Samantha had managed to hop across to the dressing table and was adding the finishing touches to her makeup as he pushed open the door. Their eyes met in the mirror.

"Nice," he approved, taking in her tomato-red silk jumpsuit and upswept hair. "If that's what you can manage in five minutes, it's just as well you overslept. Anything more glamorous would have Lilah and her friends clawing you to shreds."

"I have to do Dominic Blair justice." She gave him a shy smile. "And, besides, this didn't need…um…it was quick to put on."

"If you mean there's nothing but this between you and the outside world then I'd better sit a very long way away from you this evening." He bent and brushed her collar aside so he could drop a kiss on the exposed nape of her neck.

It was a very gentle kiss but its effect on Samantha was startling. Something inside her exploded into a molten heat that flooded her limbs and sent a visible shudder right through her body. She stared wide-eyed at his reflection in the mirror as the emotional restraints that had held her in check for so long suddenly snapped.

He raised his head and she heard his sharp intake of breath as their eyes met. For a moment they both remained motionless, then he slowly straightened up.

"Are you ready?" His voice was husky and barely controlled.

"Almost." She reached for her lip gloss. "I just need to add some war paint so I can compete downstairs."

"You don't need it." Although his voice had regained its lightness his fingertips carried a message of their own as they rested on her shoulders. "Lilah would give her eye-teeth for a complexion that doesn't come out of a bottle.

Besides, you don't have time. Our twenty minutes is almost up and I still haven't bandaged your foot."

* * *

They made it to the dining room with a minute to spare and were greeted with a round of applause.

"As a punishment for being late, you two will sit at opposite ends of the room for the rest of the evening," Lilah announced, enjoying Samantha's blushes. "Jon, you come and sit next to me, and Samantha you sit at the head of the table because you'll be doing all the talking...but not until we've had our fill of that gorgeous jumpsuit," she added, as Jonathan started to escort Samantha across the room. "It's only our complete dedication to Dominic's designs that kept us sitting here while you two indulged in bath time frolics."

"I fell asleep." Samantha's fading blushes returned to clash vividly with the tomato-red of her suit. "Jonathan had to wake me up."

"Don't spoil it, honey." Cheryl Napier, a natural redhead who had made her name appearing in an escapist adventure series as a glamorous TV cop, gave her a wide smile. "We've all been indulging in a little fantasy of our own while we've been waiting for you. After all, your photographer is the sort of man dreams are made of."

The pressure of Jonathan's fingers on her arm dispelled Samantha's momentary irritation. He was right. They had no hope of defending themselves against such a forceful group of gossips as Lilah and her friends—and, besides, there was too much truth in their accusations now for her to deny it with any real conviction. So instead of frowning, she smiled and lifted her shoulders in a shrug of confirmation, slanting a sly look at Jonathan from beneath her lashes as she did so.

He smiled down at her, his eyes telling her she was beautiful, his fingers telling her that he wanted her, and yet behind the smile she could detect a sadness tinged with anger. Her stomach lurched, inexplicably panicked as she sensed a slight withdrawal. It was too soon for her to cope with his moodiness again. She had let down too many defenses in the past hour to cope with that now.

"It's all right Samantha." His voice was barely a whisper, his lips moving infinitesimally. He didn't even look at her, as if he knew that any direct contact between them would provoke a further chorus of female sarcasm. Samantha let out her breath in relief and then slowly pirouetted, taking her weight on her good foot as Lilah demanded to see the back of her jumpsuit.

When the ladies had commented on her perfectly matching lipstick, and the huge butterfly clip that she had used to secure her damp hair into an elegant topknot, she limped across to the head of the table with a smile, and changed from Sam, the girl who was falling in love with Jonathan Aiken, to Samantha Brown, the driving force behind Dominic Blair.

"What really kept you waiting, ladies, was your burning desire to know exactly what Dominic has designed for each of you."

Her remark effectively turned the tables on them, directing their attention away from her and Jonathan to the real reason for Lilah's dinner party. Soon they were firing questions at her and discussing the proposed locations for their photographs with enthusiasm.

"Has Dominic really designed dresses specifically for each of us?" Tina Schulz, a tall, leggy brunette known for her long legs and sexy songs, produced an expectant silence with her question.

"Not exactly." Samantha relaxed into her role of fashion coordinator with an expertise born of long practice. "He chose six models with your various colorings and proportions and designed a collection of clothes for each of them, all of which we will be showing at Morton's on the first of June. After you've seen them, you can each select the outfit you like best, and once we've made any necessary alterations you'll be photographed wearing it. The dress you choose will remain your property, with Dominic's grateful thanks."

She shot Lilah a mischievous smile. "And as you all know the price of a Dominic Blair dress, I think you'll agree that you are getting a very healthy fee for your time, as well as a great deal of free publicity."

Tina gave a gravelly laugh as she flashed a suggestive smile in Jonathan's direction. "I'm not going to argue with that. I don't know about you ladies, but I'd be prepared to stand on my head naked for a Dominic Blair dress."

"I don't think that's quite the sort of publicity Samantha has in mind," Jonathan's quick repartee drew laughs from all the women at the table. He finished his coffee and stood up. "Please excuse me. Now I know everything there is to know about Dominic Blair dresses, I'll leave you to finish your discussions in peace. I've one or two telephone calls to make."

He picked up Lilah's hand and brought it to his lips in an exaggerated gesture.

"Good night, Jon." She smiled up at him, preening slightly at his attention.

"Ladies." He included them all in his smile. He didn't single out Samantha, but as his eyes met hers she was aware of a warmth in the pit of her stomach. His very reticence told her that the feeling between them was special and that he wasn't about to expose it to Lilah and her guests in case it became the butt of more jokes. She inclined her head, her cheeks flushed pink.

"Good night, Jonathan." Her voice was lost in the general chorus but she knew he had heard her. And, tomorrow, there was Malibu.

* * *

It was late when Samantha woke the following morning and she stretched luxuriously between the linen sheets. The dinner party had continued for a long time after Jonathan's departure, with Lilah and her friends swapping stories, and all of them indulging in collective self-congratulation at having been singled out by Dominic.

"Well, you each have a lot to offer." Samantha knew when compliments were the order of the day. "Tina's legs, Cheryl's hair, Lilah's figure," she smiled around the table. "Each one of you has something special."

"Don't stop." Cassie Corbière, a hard-nosed box office draw with a face like an angel gave her a wicked smile. "You've paid three compliments, now balance it up, Samantha."

"Well, your profile had Dominic designing in white and gold," Samantha returned her smile with equal wickedness. "Although he say flame red would be more fitting, did your fans but know it."

Cassie joined in the general laughter as Samantha continued her survey of the table. "Terri has given him a long-awaited chance to design for the petite woman instead of his usual

111

six-foot models." She smiled at Terri de Loren, a tiny blonde with perfect proportions who had a place in the heart of most of America's men.

"And you don't need to explain me." Bettine Cooper, the last person at the table, gave Samantha a high voltage smile. She was tall and slim, the latest attraction in a million-dollar macho film, and her skin was a smooth, velvety black with the bloom of a purple grape.

Samantha smiled as she remembered the conversation. It had been a good evening, despite her tiredness. Lilah's friends had not been the bitchy prima donnas Jonathan had predicted. They had been friendly and helpful, and she made a mental note to take him to task about it.

Take him to task. She pushed back the sheets with a smile and stretched again, not an early morning stretch but something that came from deep inside her, an anticipatory, physical response to the day ahead.

Her dreams had been insubstantial, mere whispers of promise, but enough to keep the feelings of yesterday alive, enough to persuade her that today would be a brave new beginning for her.

A cautious flexing of her foot told her that a night's rest had improved her ankle. It still hurt, but she could bear her weight on it again, and a day on the beach wasn't going to overtax it like the tour of Hollywood yesterday.

She took more trouble with her appearance than she had on the previous morning, brushing her hair hard until it flew about her head in a cloud of curls, and then securing it with a loose leather thong at the nape of her neck so that it waved and curled seductively across shoulders left bare over a brief halter top. Cotton jeans and espadrilles completed her outfit. She didn't use much makeup, just a soft peach-colored lip gloss and brown mascara, but she was satisfied with the effect against skin already lightly tanned by a day in the Los Angeles sunshine.

She added a spray of perfume and then made her way downstairs with a fast beating heart, quite sure Jonathan would be waiting on the terrace, his eyes full of promise, his hair still damp from an early morning swim.

He wasn't though, nor was he in any of the reception rooms. In fact, the whole house seemed to be empty so she made her way to the kitchen, hoping Myrna would know where everyone was.

The housekeeper was marinating a pile of inch-thick steaks while she chatted to Joe, Lilah's chauffeur-cum-handyman. They both turned and smiled as Samantha joined them.

"Did you sleep well?" Myrna broke off from her steaks long enough to pour her a cup of coffee from the percolator. "I wouldn't let Jonathan disturb you after your long day yesterday, although he wasn't pleased, but Miss Mandeville backed me up. She said that as the

113

dinner party didn't finish until well after midnight, you needed your beauty sleep. He did leave you this though."

She held out a thick brown envelope as she spoke. Samantha thanked her and then limped back to the terrace, accompanied by Joe, who settled her onto a pool lounger by adjusting the canopy so that the early morning sun wouldn't shine directly into her eyes.

"Miss Mandeville says you're to spend the day beside the pool, ma'am." He gave her a slow smile. "She'll be back by four, and she wants you to be rested enough to attend her barbecue this evening."

"Thanks, Joe." Samantha nodded gratefully and then sighed as he turned away. Lilah was certainly going to town on the entertaining, making the most of her connection with Dominic Blair.

You should be grateful, she chided herself. After all, publicity is what this trip is all about. But she knew her heart wasn't in it. Jonathan was dominating her thoughts to the exclusion of everything else. She needed to come to terms with her feelings for him so she could concentrate on Dominic Blair again. She tore open the envelope with a shiver of anticipation.

It was full of glossy prints which she tipped out onto her lap as Myrna brought her some fruit juice and a hot roll.

She nodded her thanks as she spread the prints across her knees. They were the shots

114

Jonathan had taken yesterday, and tucked in amongst them was a brief note.

I'm needed in New York. Myrna and Lilah wouldn't let me wake you, so explanations will have to wait until our date in Malibu.
Enclosed are yesterday's shots so you can make some choices while I'm away. I don't know when I'll be back so just rest that ankle of yours while you're waiting.
J.
PS. Don't go to sleep in the bath!

Chapter Six

Samantha finished reading the note with a feeling that was somewhere between laughter and disappointment. Although he mentioned Malibu, there was no other reference to what had happened between them the previous evening, only jokiness.

She sighed as she sipped her fruit juice. What else did she expect when, despite the attraction she could no longer hide, he still thought she was involved with Dominic. Malibu was the place where she was going to explain everything and now it had been taken away from her.

"Drat you, Dominic," she muttered under her breath, folding the note smoothly between her fingers and slipping it into her pocket. "Drat you and your reputation—and drat my own stupid, pig-headed pride."

The rest of the day passed slowly as Samantha lounged beside the pool in a state of depressed lethargy. Although she shuffled desultorily through the photographs and picked out the shots she liked best, she didn't bother to match them to the snippets of material she had brought with her. Any final decisions could wait. Instead, she changed into a bikini and concentrated on sunning herself, indulging in several hours of warmth and rest before Lilah returned home just after four.

"Feeling better, honey?" she greeted Samantha cheerily. "Myrna pinned my ears back this morning for keeping you up half the night. She even made Jon leave without seeing you, although when his phone call from New York came through at three this morning, I was more than a little surprised to find him in his own bedroom."

Samantha greeted this quip with a shrug and a smile before changing the subject. It worked, and by the time they left the terrace to shower and change for the barbecue, Jonathan had been forgotten as far as Lilah was concerned.

* * *

The barbecue was a great success and Samantha enjoyed herself. After a day beside the pool she felt more relaxed, and sure too that when she told Jonathan how mistaken he was about Dominic, everything would be put right between them.

Perhaps it was her newly awakened sexuality, or perhaps it was the perfect cut of her Dominic Blair sundress against the sun-kissed glow of her skin and the deeper gold of her hair, that strongly attracted Lilah's male guests. Whatever it was, she was soon surrounded by

117

admirers, several of whom were well known in the film world.

"Why don't you try for a screen test while you're in Hollywood?" one of them asked her. "With a face and figure like yours, you'll be snapped up."

"And dropped just as quickly." Samantha laughed, recognizing this as a chat up line. "I'm quite happy as I am, thank you."

"Which is fresh and unspoilt," a jaded matron in her late fifties declared ringingly. "Leave her alone, JC, because you know as well as I do that Hollywood takes natural beauties like Samantha and turns them into old hags like me."

"Nonsense." Samantha's admirer said with a note of hearty chivalry. "You're still a beautiful woman, Laura."

"I'm not, and you know it." The woman, once a household name but now only remembered from an occasional showing of her old films, scowled at him. "So don't you dare set hands on this child."

She turned back to Samantha. "Enjoy Hollywood for its fantasy, my dear, but don't stay too long. Make sure you escape back into the real world before it's too late."

"I intend to." Samantha thought of Jonathan with a frisson of pleasure because she knew he felt the same. For all his charm and sophistication at Lilah's dinner table, he was a serious and dedicated professional. He was part of her world: a world of deadlines and meetings and not enough time...except that they would find time, she knew they would, and her heart bucked against her ribs as she thought about what that meant.

* * *

The rest of the week passed in a whirl of activity as Samantha juggled making decisions about which location to use with which dresses, party invitations, and meetings with future clients. By the time Dominic arrived she was able to tell him that her early arrival in Hollywood was worth a fortune in orders.

"Lilah made sure I met everyone who matters," she explained as they sat on the terrace. "So now we've enough orders to keep us busy for months, with promises of more to come."

Lilah slipped her arm through Dominic's as he sat beside the pool, looking out across the perfection of her garden to the hills beyond. "Samantha is a priceless asset darling although I assume you already know that. As well as singlehandedly running the show, she models your dresses like nobody else. She's become quite the toast of Hollywood this week, with the men around town queuing up to escort her."

"Well what do you know, my little sister has the makings of a star," Dominic teased, but he didn't sound his usual enthusiastic self.

Samantha raised her eyebrows in a question. He shook his head, his eyes momentarily flicking across to Sally Bowman who had accompanied him on the flight out.

Samantha's eyes widened. So that was the trouble. She had noticed that Sally was very quiet but had assumed it was because she didn't know Lilah or any of the other people on the terrace. She glanced across to where the makeup artist sat toying with an almost-full glass of champagne, ignoring the small talk that was going on around her. She looked ill, her naturally pale complexion almost drained of color beside all the Californian suntans. Even her hair had lost its luster, fading to a dull, rusty red instead of its usual vibrant auburn.

She looked back at Dominic. He was laughing again, his teeth very even and white against the darkness of his tan, charming Lilah and her friends with compliments; but Samantha noticed that the laughter didn't reach his eyes and, as she watched, she saw him glance at Sally several more times.

Something was going on and now wasn't the time for it, not when they needed to concentrate on their Hollywood venture. It was bad enough that she was falling for Jonathan, without Dominic and Sally causing difficulties as well. After all, they were the two most directly involved with the models, so any temperamental outbursts on their part would have repercussions on the overall mood of the fashion show.

She got up and walked across to where Sally was sitting. Her foot was almost better now so she was wearing high-heeled sandals again. Sally looked up when she heard the clicking of Samantha's heels against the pink and gray tiles.

"Are you enjoying yourself?" Samantha sank into a vacant chair.

"Yes, it was very kind of Lilah to include me in her house party," Sally's voice was a monotone, her usually sparkling eyes dead.

"Is something wrong?" Samantha pushed aside her own worries and concentrated on the girl in front of her. This wasn't the Sally she had come to know so well during the past few months. Her vibrancy and enthusiasm had gone and she exuded unhappiness.

When Sally remained silent, Samantha looked across to where Dominic was standing, searching for a clue to her odd behavior. Then her heart did a somersault because Dominic wasn't alone. He was talking to Jonathan. They were shaking hands, nodding, agreeing about something, and then Jonathan turned, his eyes skimming Lilah's guests, searching.

She smiled, half rose from her seat, her lips dry with anticipation. This was the moment to show him that he was wrong about Dominic, the moment to show him how she really felt. She forgot about Lilah, forgot about the other guests, forgot everyone but Jonathan. Everything else faded away as he came towards her, his hair ruffled by the evening breeze, his crumpled shirt and cotton jeans evidence that he had come to the party straight from the airport.

For a second their eyes met, and then his gaze slipped past her to where Sally was sitting. Her smile fixed, Samantha hesitated, wondering why he looked so tired, wishing she could ask him. And while she hesitated, Sally left her chair and stepped forward, and when Jonathan opened his arms, she stepped into them with a harsh, dry sob.

After that, the party broke up. Sally's obvious emotion was too raw for Lilah's guests so they soon made excuses to leave. Dominic and Samantha sat alone on the terrace as Lilah waved everyone off from her semicircular driveway.

Jonathan and Sally had disappeared without a word to anyone, their arms around one another, Sally's head resting on his shoulder.

As she watched them walk away Samantha's heart seemed to stop beating although she knew she was still alive because everything hurt. Her eyes, her throat, the empty space deep in her chest—they all ached unbearably. Her mouth felt stretched and sore from the constant smiling farewells. It wouldn't have been so bad if Jonathan had smiled at her, but he hadn't, not even the merest flicker.

She glanced across at Dominic. He looked white and drawn and was tapping his fingers repeatedly against the arm of his chair.

"Dominic," she whispered, her throat thick with unshed tears, "tell me what's going on."

Her words brought him back to the present. He forced a smile.

"I don't know, Sam. I arranged to travel over with Sally and then, a few days before the flight, she telephoned to tell me she had to go to New York right away. She didn't say why but we arranged to meet at Los Angeles airport so I was sure she would tell me then. She didn't though. She just looked desolate and we travelled all the way to Lilah's house in a terrible despairing silence. I tried everything I could think of as we drove out here, but she didn't even seem to be listening to me. She's locked up with some terrible hurt and she won't share it with me.

"It's made me realize how I feel about her. I just want to comfort her and I've never wanted to hold any of my girlfriends like that before. But she won't let me near her. I know my reputation doesn't give me the aura of a dependable protector, but I thought she liked me enough to confide in me. Apparently not though. I think I might have thrown something very precious away before I even realized its value."

"Jonathan has just come back from New York." Samantha's eyes reflected Dominic's pain. "He had a telephone call a few days ago and left here at the crack of dawn without explaining why."

"You too, Sam." Dominic knew her too well not to understand the huskiness in her voice. "Has he really broken into that cold little heart of yours?"

She nodded as she attempted to smile through her tears. "There still a saving grace, though. He thinks I'm having an affair with you. He doesn't know you're my stepbrother. I didn't have time to tell him before he went to New York, and now..."

"Now you don't want him to know." Dominic took her hand in both of his. "Don't worry, love, I shan't say a word. And it's such an accepted fact in the fashion world that nobody else is likely to mention it, either."

"Thank you." Samantha moved across to where he was sitting. "About Sally, Dominic. At one time I really thought you two were going to make it you know."

"And we might have done if I hadn't been such a commitment phobe that I wouldn't admit to what was happening to me." Dominic took hold of her hand as they watched the sun fade behind the distant hills. "We haven't learned much about the art of living, have we, Sam? I had too much, too soon, and thought the world would always jump to my bidding; you lost too much, too soon so were scared to face real life again. If I hadn't been so self-absorbed I could

124

have helped you, then perhaps this hurt wouldn't have cut so deep."

"Yes, it would." Samantha's voice was muffled. "Jonathan would have affected me this way whenever I met him. But it's over now. I have to bury him along with Danny and start again."

"Poor Sam." Dominic turned his face towards her, the sadness in his eyes for them both. As he leaned across to give her a sympathetic, brotherly kiss on the cheek, Jonathan walked across the terrace.

"Lilah wants to know if you are joining us for coffee?" His voice was cold, his eyes expressionless in the fading light.

"No, thank you." Dominic tightened his fingers on Samantha's hand and shook his head. "I'm for bed. How about you, sweetie?" He turned back to Samantha with a possessive smile. "Are you tired?"

Ignoring Jonathan, Samantha nodded.

"In that case, would you give Lilah our apologies." Dominic stood up, his fingers still entwined in Samantha's, and looked directly at Jonathan.

"As you wish." He said, his eyes hard as they rested on Samantha.

She stared back at him defiantly. How dare he treat her so coldly after everything that had happened between them. How dare he insult her by ignoring her when he first arrived. She held her head high as she and Dominic walked towards the house, and kept it proudly in position until they reached her room.

"Are you okay?" Dominic's hand was sympathetic on her arm. "I came all the way just in case he decided to watch us."

"Thank you." Samantha gave him a tired smile. "It's a silly deception, really. Childish, unworthy of me, and one easily destroyed by a chance word from Lilah or Sally, but it's all I've got to make life bearable right now."

"Then you've one thing more than me." Dominic's eyes were dark with pain as he tried to smile. "Because all I've got is the knowledge that everything is my fault. Six months ago Sally was mine for the asking, and I wouldn't commit myself. Now she's made it clear that it's far too late."

* * *

Breakfast was a very silent affair the following morning, with everyone hiding behind dark glasses as Myrna bustled from kitchen to terrace and back again. Jonathan and Dominic managed eggs and hash browns while the women toyed silently with orange juice and coffee. Conversation was desultory and confined solely to the weather and items of news.

Finally, Jonathan pushed back his chair and got up. Samantha watched him, her fingernails cutting sharply into her tightly clenched palms.

It was the first time she had dared to look directly at him and it did her no good at all. He was still tall and slim, he still moved with that arrogant lazy grace. Only his eyes were different as they met hers. They were so cold that she felt like a fly impaled on a pin, each moment increasing her agony.

"What did you think of the photos?" She jumped when he spoke, his voice clipped and formal.

"They…they were very good." She looked away, not wanting to betray herself, and deciding she needed Dominic's support, turned to him. "We thought we'd spend the morning making our final selection, didn't we?

He nodded. "You are welcome to join us but I imagine you have better things to do."

"As it happens, I have." He held out his hand. "Coming, Sally?"

She jumped up with a smile. Although her face was still pale she looked considerably better, as if Jonathan's arrival last night had dispelled some of her unhappiness. Samantha stared after them as they walked towards the house, pausing briefly beside Lilah's chair. How was she going to cope for the next few days? The impending fashion show meant they would all have to work very closely together, exchanging ideas, adapting to one another's needs. Was she going to be able to do that while she was nursing a broken heart?

127

Only twenty-four hours earlier she had been counting every moment, knowing that Jonathan must return by the twenty-eighth, anxious to explain everything to him, commit herself, and all the time he had been stringing her along, while he waited for Sally to arrive. His offer on the observation floor at City Hall had obviously been the true one despite all his later protestations. He just wanted to enjoy a short affair, taking each day as it came, no commitments, no responsibility, until Sally arrived. He wasn't bothered about her supposed relationship with Dominic at all. He just wanted to play the field.

Maybe that was why Sally had been so unhappy when she arrived. Maybe she had heard a rumor of the silly gossip that Lilah had started and it had taken his actual presence to convince her that Samantha meant nothing to him at all.

It didn't explain everything, though. It didn't explain why they had both gone to New York, nor did it explain the extent of their relationship: whether it was new, or long-standing, or even something from the past that a chance meeting had re-established. Nor did she understand Sally's uncharacteristic coolness towards Dominic.

She sighed, and drained her coffee. Whatever was happening, sitting here wasn't going to help. The only thing that would rescue her and Dominic from their unhappiness was work. It had helped in the past and it would help again.

"Come on, Domino." Instinctively, she used his childhood nickname, knowing that by using it he would sense her affection and sympathy. "We've a lot of work to do and not much time."

"You're such a slave driver." He forced some enthusiasm into his voice as he scraped back his chair. "Can we use your dining room, Lilah? We need a lot of table space and no distractions."

"Help yourselves." Lilah waved a nonchalant hand in the direction of the house. "Nobody will disturb you until lunchtime."

"In that case, I'll go upstairs and fetch the artwork." Dominic gave them both a strained smile as he made for the house.

"Samantha." Lilah's voice was sharp as Samantha made to follow him. She turned back with a sigh, knowing what was on the older woman's mind.

"What's with you and Jonathan, honey?" Lilah removed her sunglasses, her eyes accusing. "A few days ago, rooms lit up when you two were around. Now, nothing—except that tear-stained redhead whose only good point is that she's cut Dominic's ego down to manageable proportions."

"I'm afraid the torch burned out, Lilah." Samantha tried for a jokey response even while she admired the other woman's shrewdness. She might appear shallow and self-absorbed but nothing of importance escaped her, not even Dominic's interest in Sally.

"Is that all you're going to say?" Lilah raised perfectly arched eyebrows. "Because if it is, let me tell you I don't believe one word of it. I've worked my way through too many relationships not to know the real thing when I see it. You and Jonathan had something special going for you, something that I'd almost forgotten existed in this fantasy world of mine. So are you going to sit back and let Sally take him away from you just because she seems to have some sort of emotional hold over him, or are you going to get out there and fight?"

Samantha sank onto the end of Lilah's lounger in surprise. "I never thought of it like that."

Suddenly she found herself pouring everything out, talking in a way she hadn't done for years, not since she was a schoolgirl agonizing with her friends in the cozy intimacy of her bedroom.

Lilah listened silently, her expression thoughtful, until Samantha's description of her supposed relationship with Dominic brought a short laugh.

"Well done! At least you're beginning to fight."

Samantha shook her head. "No, I'm not. It was just a silly misunderstanding that I didn't have time to put right."

"A fortunate omission under the circumstances." Lilah showed her teeth in a smile of appreciation. "Now, I want you to tell me just one thing, and I want you to be completely truthful. Are you in love with Jonathan Aiken?"

"I thought I was, even though common sense told me it was too soon," Samantha looked away, concentrating on a single leaf that was floating slowly across the surface of the pool. "But that was before Sally arrived and I realized how stupid it was to even consider such a thing."

The lounger moved as Lilah leaned forward. "People don't fall out of love as soon as someone lets them down, Samantha. If they did, then the world would be a very much happier place because there wouldn't be hundreds of lonely, rejected people wondering where it all went wrong. So let me give you another chance to answer my question. Are you in love with Jonathan?"

"If you put it like that, then yes, I am." Samantha turned and faced her, angry tears brimming in her eyes. "I'd give anything not to be because it hurts like mad, but yes, I'm in love with him."

Lilah replaced her sunglasses with a satisfied smile. "Good, now we're getting somewhere. And believe me, honey, I know every trick in the book. I also know Jon better than he knows himself. He's not really interested in Dominic's girlfriend. Maybe she is someone from his past who won't let him go, or maybe he's using her to hurt you because he thinks you're involved with Dominic. With Jonathan, you can never tell. He's a law unto himself and always has been, ever since he was a child."

"You've known him that long?" Samantha's eyes widened. "But I thought…" She stopped abruptly, and blushed.

"You thought I'd had an affair with him." Lilah relaxed into a gale of laughter. "I'm flattered, of course, darling, but I don't think his father would have approved. I was Jonathan's stepmother for a short while, way back in the early days of my film career when I needed to be married to a film director with influence."

She grinned at Samantha's incredulous expression. "Surely you've heard of Arnold Aiken? When he was alive he collected starlets like other people collect butterflies. That's why Jonathan is the way he is. He was only six when I first met him, and even then he gave nothing away because too many hopeful stars had tried to use him to get to his father. It's an experience that has left him with a great contempt for the human race in general, and Hollywood celebrities in particular."

"That explains a lot." Samantha stared at her in surprise. "I couldn't understand why he didn't want this assignment, especially once I realized how well he knows Hollywood."

"The place holds too many painful memories," Lilah said, her face serious for a moment. Then she laughed and changed the subject. "And you better feel flattered that I've given you such intimate details of my private life because once you know that Jon is thirty-three, you won't find it too hard to work out my age, give or take a year or two."

"I won't tell." Samantha was surprised to find that she could still smile.

"Well, if it ever gets out, I'll know who to blame," Lilah leaned back and closed her eyes. "Now go and find Dominic and work your frustration out of your system. I'm going to have a nap."

"But what do I have to do?" Samantha stared at Lilah's closed eyes, surprised that their conversation had ended so abruptly.

"You don't have to do anything." Lilah pushed up her sunglasses again and squinted into the sun. "Just keep up the pretense with Dominic, and I will take care of everything else."

* * *

It didn't take Samantha long to work out what Lilah meant, because when they all met for a cold lunch on the terrace she was wearing the briefest of bikinis and smoothing suntan oil onto her legs.

133

"Please help me, darling," she appealed huskily to Dominic as he strolled across the pink and gray tiles. "I need some oil on my back."

"My pleasure." He knelt obediently beside her chair and waited for her to roll over before rubbing the oil into her skin with long, sensuous strokes.

Samantha watched them suspiciously. Although she hadn't mentioned her conversation with Lilah, something told her that Dominic knew what their hostess was up to and was playing along with her for all he was worth. She sighed. If only she had concentrated more on living and relationships, and less on her work, she might understand what was going on.

Dominic, on the other hand, seemed to be enjoying himself. His fingers lingered more with each stroke and his mouth was close to Lilah's ear as they shared a whispered conversation. Samantha watched in admiration. Whatever Lilah was up to, she certainly had the equipment to achieve it. She didn't look close to her age, and at a time when most women start to think about one-piece swimsuits, she did something for her brief bikini that made Samantha feel positively envious.

She turned away to help herself to food from the cold buffet Myrna had prepared for their lunch, and found Jonathan staring at her. He was sitting next to Sally, his arm along the back of her chair, and the scornful curl of his lip told Samantha that he was waiting for her to react as Dominic and Lilah continued to giggle beside the pool.

She returned his stare with equal scorn and then piled some meat and salad onto her plate and took them to a chair in a patch of shade, well away from the rest of them. Behind her she could hear Sally chatting. The color had returned to her face during the morning and she was talking normally with Jonathan, her voice light and confident.

Samantha listened bitterly. She couldn't make out the words, only the general, intimate tone of the conversation. It sounded rather one-sided though, as if Sally was doing all the talking, and she wondered again about Lilah's remarks. Was she right in thinking that Sally was just someone from Jonathan's past who had an emotional claim on him?

Stop it, she told herself sharply. Lilah is wrong. One look at the bloom that had been restored to Sally's cheeks made that very clear. Whatever it is that Lilah thinks she is doing is a waste of time. I need to forget Jonathan even if I can't stop loving him. Some things are just not meant to be and when I get her on her own I'm going to tell her so.

She forced herself to relax and continued to eat her salad until a scraping of chairs signaled that Lilah and Dominic had finished their games and joined Jonathan and Sally at the table. After a moment she became acutely aware that she was sitting alone while the rest of them chatted together, apparently amicably. She felt uncomfortable. It must look as if she was sulking, as if she cared about Jonathan's defection to Sally and that was the last thing she wanted him to think.

Then she realized it wasn't that at all. Lilah had deliberately set things up so it looked as if Samantha was sulking about her flirtation with Dominic. So that was what she was up to. She was trying to make Jonathan angry, trying to make him think that she and Dominic were making a fool of Samantha. She was trying to sting him into some sort of reaction that would uncover his true allegiance, and she was obviously hoping, at the same time, to make Sally aware of Dominic once again.

She turned in her chair, wondering whether she should rejoin the others and dismiss her apparent sulkiness with a joke, or whether she should let Lilah carry on, but then it was too late to do anything because Jonathan was standing beside her, holding out a glass of wine.

"You forgot to pour yourself one." He handed it to her, his eyes half-closed against the sun, his expression impossible to read.

"Thank you." She accepted the drink politely, avoiding his fingers.

He nodded and then pulled up a chair and sat astride it, leaving his own wine untouched on the ground beside him.

"I'm sorry I had to leave so abruptly the other day. A friend was in trouble so I didn't have any choice."

"You don't need to explain." Samantha's voice sounded small and cold as she remembered again that Sally had been in New York as well. "You're not employed by Dominic Blair, Jonathan. You work for *Elite* so you only have to answer to them."

"That's not what I meant and you know it." He turned his head sharply, his eyes no longer cold but blazing hot. But before he could continue, before Samantha had time to register the furious beating of her heart, Dominic interrupted them.

"Come along, you two." It was the old sexy, devilish Dominic speaking as he seized Samantha's hands. "Lilah says we must all go swimming. She says the pool hasn't been used enough recently."

"Count me out." Jonathan straightened up from his chair with a shake of his head. "I've already promised to take Sally shopping this afternoon. She needs a few items for her makeup tray."

He turned away as he finished speaking and strode back to the table without a backward glance, leaving Dominic and Samantha alone. They stared forlornly at one another, although Dominic kept up a line of banter until he was out of earshot.

Samantha finally put out her hand. "Don't Dominic. This silly pretense doesn't seem such a good idea after all."

"Don't you dare give up," Lilah's voice was a fierce whisper as she joined them. "Trust me, the pair of you. You're like a couple of babes in arms as far as real relationships are concerned. Now come on, into the pool, and for goodness' sake look as if you're enjoying yourselves."

Chapter Seven

It seemed to Samantha that she spent every minute of the next four days trying to look as if she were enjoying herself. On Lilah's instructions, Dominic made sure Jonathan never had a chance to be alone with her, and as they shared adjoining bedrooms, he couldn't even know that they slept in separate beds. But while she ensured that Samantha was always chaperoned, Lilah also attached herself permanently to Dominic, so they appeared to be a scandalous trio, with Samantha giving every appearance of accepting the situation without a fight.

If it had any effect on Jonathan and Sally, they didn't show it. Instead they spent more and more time together, using the pool when the others vacated it, sitting on the terrace when everyone else went inside. Finally, Samantha could stand it no longer.

"For goodness' sake, you two," she confronted Lilah and Dominic in exasperation. "We can't go on like this forever. Besides,

Jonathan and Sally don't even notice. They're quite happy with their own company."

"That's where you're wrong." Lilah dropped her seductive pout and smiled knowingly. "Jonathan is getting angrier by the minute."

* * *

Despite the tangle of their emotional life, Samantha and Dominic still managed to get a lot of work done. They visited Morton's with Lilah and checked the details for the fashion show, and then spent hours pressing the numerous outfits that Dominic had brought with him. When they were finished, they hung the clothes on a series of extending travel rails in one of the spare bedrooms until the room was a crazy kaleidoscope of strong primary colors in an exotic mixture of silk, cotton, and the finest wool.

They surveyed the scene before them with satisfaction. It was the result of months of hard work, and the culmination of their ambitions to date. From this should come a new level of fame, a new demand for their clothes.

"Has it been worth it?" Samantha asked, remembering the late nights and the frayed tempers with a wry smile.

Dominic nodded slowly. "There's only one thing missing—someone to share it with. Other than you, I mean," he added, draping his arm around her shoulders.

She frowned up at him. "Do you think Lilah's plan is working, Dominic?"

"Search me." He gave a tired shrug. "I can't think straight anymore. I thought I knew everything there was to know about women, about what I wanted out of life. Now I know I don't know anything, and Sally looks right through me as if I don't exist. She's polite enough, even friendly, but disinterested, only really lighting up for Jonathan."

At the mention of his name, Samantha turned away and concentrated on smoothing out the folds of a dress. After that they didn't discuss it anymore but threw themselves into making the final arrangements for the fashion show. They also agreed the locations for the magazine coverage. This involved several discussions with Jonathan as well as another pile of proofs, which this time included the front of the Gucci shop in exclusive Rodeo Drive as well as some shots along Sunset Boulevard with several strategically placed high end cars and imposing gateways dominating the pictures.

There were also two sets of new shots from City Hall, one with the sun lower in the sky. In it, Los Angeles seemed a fantasy city drifting on a rose-colored cloud.

"He's good." Dominic threw the photos back onto the table with a scowl. "The man with everything. Looks, money, talent and the woman I love."

"You could almost be describing yourself," Samantha answered as she leafed through the proofs, checking their final decisions.

Dominic pushed back his chair and walked across to the window, his hands thrust moodily into his pockets. After a moment, Samantha joined him, and they stared down at the pool area where Sally lay sunning herself while Jonathan swam lazily up and down.

"A keep-fit fanatic too," Dominic muttered, then he pushed himself away from the window and made purposefully for the door. "I've had enough of this, Sam. I'm going down there to talk to Sally whether she likes it or not. Once we really did have something going for us so I'm not prepared to let her pretend it never happened a moment longer."

He banged the door shut behind him and reappeared on the terrace a few moments later, just as Jonathan emerged from the pool. The two men nodded coldly to one another and then paused for a brief conversation before Jonathan looked towards the house. Samantha drew back into the shadows but she was too slow. She knew he had seen her watching him.

She was still fighting the memory of his almost-naked body when the door opened and he entered the room, a towel slung across his shoulders and his brief swimming trunks replaced by a pair of blue shorts.

"I thought you might like these." He threw a brown envelope onto the table. It spilled open, scattering prints onto the polished surface. They were the pictures he had taken of Samantha on her first day in Hollywood, the ones she knew about as well as a whole lot more, snapped when she was unaware of his camera.

"Thank you." She picked them up one by one, remembering each moment with a stabbing sensation in her heart. Here she was laughing outside the Chinese Theatre, and in this one she was gazing solemnly along the Walk of Fame. There were pictures of her entering the Brown Derby, and some of her sitting patiently on a low wall, waiting for Jonathan, and then those taken at City Hall with the sprawl of Los Angeles in the background.

She turned them over methodically, embarrassed by the memories they recalled, searching for a casual remark that would put things into perspective. It remained unuttered, however, as she reached the last print—a close-up of her face as she looked across at Jonathan. The photograph revealed her feelings for him completely. Her eyes were wide and luminous, her lips slightly parted, the expression on her face part puzzled, part hopeful. Hastily she added it to the pile, but she was too late. Jonathan took a step forward and picked it up.

"Disturbs you, does it?" He held it out to her, his eyes scornful as they flickered across her face. "You prefer life to be comfortable,

143

don't you Samantha? No unwelcome emotions, nothing that will rock the boat."

"I don't know what you're talking about." She pushed the other photographs back into the envelope, trying to disguise the fact that her hands were shaking.

"You're very good at burying your head in the sand, aren't you?" He tossed the photograph across to her and then leaned forward, resting both his hands on the table. "You can't ignore what that photograph says as easily as you ignore Dominic's behavior, because the camera doesn't lie. Don't you care that he's making a fool of you, or are you so used to it that it has ceased to matter? Does nothing matter except your job? Is your job so important that you are prepared to forgive him anything, put up with every disloyalty, as long as he continues to return to you? Are you really going to carry on selling your soul, Samantha?"

"I don't see what business it is of yours," Samantha was pale as she faced him. "After all, you went off to New York with barely a word, and then Sally ran straight into your arms when you returned, so you can hardly talk about loyalty. Does she know about your attempts to seduce me? Is that why she was so miserable when she first arrived? I know you were both in New York together, so don't try to deny it.

"Whatever are you talking about?" He moved away from the table and came towards her, his brows drawn together in a frown. "What

144

did you expect me to do when I arrived in the middle of Lilah's party—sweep you into my arms in front of Dominic? In case you've forgotten, he's your partner, and whatever I might think of his behavior, and of you for putting up it, I wasn't about to make him look foolish in front of Lilah's guests.

"Besides, I wasn't even sure about your feelings for me after five days apart. You were so elusive, so noncommittal, that part of me wondered whether the feelings between us were a figment of my imagination. It has taken that photograph to show me the truth. I barely glanced at it when it was developed because I was in such a hurry to fly to New York. Today, when I found it in a drawer, I was knocked sideways by the expression on your face."

He had continued to walk round the table while he was speaking and now he towered over her, his eyes fierce.

"Have you forgotten how you felt, Samantha, because if you have I'll remind you."

"No!" Too late she realized his intention but she was trapped between the table and the window and all she could do was turn her head away and bring her arms up between them as he reached for her.

"Yes!" The word was an explosion of sound as he lowered his head, his eyes steely grey against a shaft of sunlight, his mouth inexorable as it searched for hers.

At first she struggled, twisting her head away, hating him for his anger and contempt; but he followed her every movement, invading her mouth and her mind until she was swept into a world of pure sensation, the only reality his skin under her fingers, his hands biting through the thin cotton of her dress. She moaned softly, a tiny involuntary sound at the back of her throat, but it was enough for Jonathan to lift his head from hers.

"Convinced, or do you need more persuasion?" He was breathing heavily, his face flushed under hair still damp from his swim.

The note of contempt in his voice brought Samantha to her senses. This wasn't what she wanted. It didn't matter anymore that Jonathan thought he was fighting Dominic; it didn't even matter about Sally and his deception. The very fact that he thought a kiss was enough to convince her of the supposed error of her ways, repelled her.

She felt bruised, violated. There was more to a relationship than that. He was only offering her half of himself; the rest had been locked away since childhood if Lilah could be believed. But that was the important half, the part of him that Samantha had glimpsed occasionally, the part she had wanted to commit herself to, not this.

She balled her hands into fists and pushed against his chest. "Let me go. It will take a lot more than a few kisses to convince me that there's any difference between you and Dominic, if you must know. You both seem to think that sex is the answer to everything."

Jonathan's face darkened as his hands dropped to his sides, freeing her so she could move away from him.

"Very observant." A mirthless smile crossed his face as their eyes met. "Tell yourself that tonight, Samantha, when you're tossing and turning in bed, wondering how much longer you have to lie there before Dominic deigns to join you. Try and forget those kisses then, and see how successful you are."

Although she slammed the door on his words, Samantha had heard them all, and she knew he was right. He was indeed going to be very hard to forget in the middle of the night.

* * *

By lunchtime all the models had arrived, and after that Samantha had very little time to worry about her reactions to Jonathan, or his involvement with Sally, because none of the girls had been rehearsed, or even seen the clothes they were to model. They were all freelance professionals, used to hard work and instantly adaptable, however, something that was quickly apparent.

"It'll be great to wear something bright for a change." Chrissie D'Arcy, a slim blonde, grinned across at Samantha. "This year it's all white, black and grey. Very depressing."

"You'll look wonderful in the blue range," Samantha assured her, remembering the hours Dominic had agonized over pictures of models, looking for the right face to model the dresses he had designed with the petite Terri de Loren in mind.

Each model had been chosen for her similarity to a film star; not to achieve an exact likeness but so that the dresses the celebrities chose would be modeled to the best effect. And now, as Samantha gave a final check to the contents of the van before locking the rear doors carefully behind her, she felt a tremendous sense of achievement. The Hollywood Collection had been an enormous challenge, wedged as it was between their regular fashion shows, and with most of the planning having to be done by phone. She hoped fervently that it would be a success. It had to be, or she and Dominic had nothing at all.

Dominic. She turned and watched him. He was talking to the models, his hands expressive as he demonstrated the imaginary swirl of a dress, a suggested pirouette. He appeared totally involved, briefing the girls on what he required from them on the catwalk, and they were listening, sober-faced, an occasional question showing their professionalism. When he finished he turned to Sally and the hairdresser who was standing beside her.

"You two can take over now," he said, showing all his teeth in a typical Dominic Blair publicity smile that gave nothing away.

With a nod of thanks, they led the girls inside the house, promising that they would all arrive a good half an hour before the show, fully made up and with every hair in place.

Dominic caught Samantha's questioning glance as he swung himself into the van but there was no time for conversation.

Samantha blinked hard, damming the threatened flood of tears, and turned back towards the house. She had promised to follow Dominic in one of Lilah's cars, and Myrna was coming too, anxious not to miss any of the excitement. She was waiting beside the main door, her hair newly set, her lipstick bright.

"I won't be a moment." Samantha took the stairs two at a time, needing to collect her bag and a few necessary items to cope with the inevitable repairs. It took only a few minutes and then she paused before the mirror, checking her own appearance carefully, aware that she needed to look every inch an advertisement for Dominic Blair.

She had chosen a pastel color, a mint green silk that wouldn't clash with the vivid colors of the Hollywood Collection. She was aware that she looked her best. The soft material clung to her, revealing curves that were a complete anathema to the models who would be surrounding her, while the green color brought a

149

delicate bloom to cheeks now tanned a warm honey color by the Californian sun. She had swept her hair off her face, and up into a fashionable tangle of curls, anxious to give herself height amongst the tall models.

She gave a nod of satisfaction, ignoring the faint shadows beneath her eyes. Sally wasn't the only one who knew how to deceive the eye with cosmetics. The effects of a lot of sleepless nights and disturbing dreams were hidden behind blusher and eye shadow.

As she turned away from the mirror her attention was caught by a movement through the half-open doorway. Jonathan and Sally were standing at the far end of the corridor outside her room, and Jonathan had his arms around Sally's waist.

Samantha froze, unable to move or make a sound, or even look away. As she watched, Sally put her hand up and patted Jonathan's cheek. She was alight with laughter and she shook her head as he spoke to her. Although Samantha couldn't see his expression, because he was half-turned away from the door, she could see the answering happiness in Sally's eyes. Then, as she watched, Jonathan tightened his hold on Sally's waist and lifted her off the ground until their faces were level. He kissed her full on the mouth before letting her slide back to the ground. As soon as her feet touched the carpet, she twisted out of his arms and ran off, laughing, and shouting something as she went, but Samantha couldn't hear what she said. She could hardly see either because tears blinded her vision and a lump in her throat made speech impossible.

So much for Jonathan's recent kiss in the dining room. So much for Lilah's assurance that he wasn't interested in Sally. Nobody could persuade her that there was nothing between them now.

* * *

Lilah had helped Samantha organize the whole fashion show with a style and panache that could only be found in Hollywood. She had produced a professional Master of Ceremonies as well as a white-tie-and-tails string quartet. The whole proceedings were to be relayed by a loudspeaker system that was rather overpowering in the genteel wicker-and-fern decor that made Morton's different from the usual Beverly Hills eating house. The owner, who played on the fact that he was British by charging outrageous prices for wafer-thin cucumber sandwiches and English tea, had made it the place to be seen in if you were anyone at all.

By four thirty it was full, with an impressive array of expensive cars lining the driveway. Behind improvised screens, helping the models to put the finishing touches to their first outfits, Dominic and Samantha could hear

151

the rising murmur outside as more and more of the Hollywood elite sat and waited.

At four thirty, at a nod from Dominic, the Master of Ceremonies interrupted the string quartet with an announcement.

"Ladies—" he paused,"—and gentlemen." There was a ripple of laughter and a smattering of applause as he included the occasional husband and a few hairdressers who had been brought along by their wealthy clients. "You will find some of Dominic Blair's business cards on your table. Put one in your handbag because Dominic will only be here until the end of the week."

He waited until the ensuing rustle had ceased and then proceeded to give them a potted version of Dominic's career and his involvement with Hollywood via one of Lilah's films. This was the cue for her to appear at the head of a long sweep of stairs. She was wearing a slinky dress of peach-colored satin with a matching cape, and she looked fabulous. A sigh went up from the women present while Jonathan and several local photographers pointed their cameras at her as she descended onto the catwalk.

Dominic was waiting for her, and he kissed her hand like a long-lost lover instead of someone who had been talking to her only five minutes earlier.

Samantha gave a wry smile. Whatever else Dominic hadn't got, he had a certain style that would never let him down. She turned away as he greeted the assembled audience, waxing enthusiastically over Lilah's part in the proceedings, describing the theme of the fashion show, and drawing envious sighs as he mentioned the names of the film stars who were to be photographed wearing his dresses for *Elite*.

Several of the models smiled at her, aware that she was more nervous than they were. To them the fashion show was just another afternoon's work, albeit a pleasant one because they liked the professional attitude of Dominic Blair compared with some of the other fashion houses. But to Samantha and Dominic it was a big part of their future.

"It's going to be fine," Chrissie pressed Samantha's hand as she walked past her and out onto the improvised catwalk.

She was soon proved right as each new outfit was greeted with loud applause and a murmur of excitement. Soon Dominic was struggling to be heard as he described each new creation amidst a plethora of popping flashbulbs as overenthusiastic local photographers vied with each other for the best shots.

Only Jonathan remained disinterested, taking several pictures of each new outfit as the model emerged onto the catwalk and then retiring to his seat beside Sally to resume what seemed to be a serious and intimate conversation.

Samantha looked across to where Lilah was sitting and wondered at her own stupidity. How could she have possibly believed that Lilah was doing anything except bolstering her own self-esteem when she insisted that they keep up such a silly pretense. She had a reputation for captivating younger men and Dominic's misery had probably seemed like a godsend to her because he was undeniably attractive as well as in need of solace. To do her justice, she had possibly meant some good to come from the whole deception. After all, Jonathan had reacted angrily, as she had predicted—but for so short a time before he returned to Sally, that Samantha no longer knew what to think about anything at all.

She was still pondering when Chrissie tapped her on the shoulder. With a start, she became aware of a tremendous burst of applause.

"Look, Dominic wants you to join him." Chrissie pushed her forward. "The whole show has been a great success and now it's your turn to take a bow."

"Me? I don't think so," Samantha shook her head in confusion. "Publicity is Dominic's side of the business, not mine."

Before she had time to protest any further, however, Dominic darted behind the screen and seized her hand. "Come on, Sam," he whispered. "It's time you stepped into the

154

limelight for once. The Hollywood Collection was your idea after all."

"No, Dominic." Samantha pulled back, suddenly panic-stricken, not because of the audience or the publicity but because Jonathan was out there and she didn't want to face the blank lens of his prying camera.

"Don't be silly. Everyone is waiting for you—and, besides, I have a few things to say."

* * *

The applause intensified as they joined Lilah at the center of the catwalk so it was some moments before Dominic could make himself heard. When he did, however, he was lavish in his praise.

"I only have to cope with the pleasant side of the business," he explained amidst a murmur of laughter. "Samantha is the person who puts everything together. Without her attention to detail, and her bossiness—" he paused for another wave of laughter, "—my fashion shows wouldn't get off the ground. As an assistant, she is invaluable—and if any of you would like an appointment with me, then I'd advise you to consult her because she's the one who makes sure I turn up on time, and with the right brief."

He grinned and then turned his hands outwards and upwards in a gesture of mock despair. "Mind you, as a sister she can sometimes be a trial. Sibling bossiness is not

155

always as welcome. I remember when I was thirteen and she was eight…" He launched into a spirited description of one of their childhood arguments, setting just the right tone, his comments humorous and entertaining.

Samantha, however, wasn't listening. She had a fixed smile on her face but her head was in a whirl. Why on earth had Dominic chosen this moment to announce their relationship? Not that it was a secret, of course, not in the fashion industry, but neither was it something they normally referred to. So why now, with Jonathan listening? Had he forgotten, in the excitement of his success, that keeping up the deception was important to her? Had he forgotten about Jonathan?

When Dominic seized her hand, she realized he had finished talking and was taking a final bow. She joined him, smiling automatically, but when he saw the anger in her eyes, and the hurt, he squeezed her hand reassuringly.

"I had to do it, Sam," he mouthed over the clamor of applause. "Believe me, if I hadn't you would never have forgiven me."

Chapter Eight

Although Samantha smiled and bowed like a puppet on a string, she never once looked in Jonathan's direction. She wouldn't give him the satisfaction of knowing why she had hidden the truth of her relationship with Dominic.

When the applause finally died away Dominic was surrounded by admirers and reporters. Busy answering questions and posing for photographs, he didn't have time to speak to Samantha, so she couldn't ask him why he'd betrayed her.

Excusing herself from the melee she hurried behind the screen to where the models were changing back into their own clothes. With Myrna's help, she began to hang the dresses back onto the rails, buttoning and zipping them tidily onto hangers.

It didn't take long but she strung it out as much as she could to avoid having to return to a restaurant still thick with photographers. She was just refolding a pile of silk scarves when Lilah appeared behind the screens, her face alight with enthusiasm.

"I'm throwing an impromptu party back at the house." Her eyes were bright, her voice a shade too loud. "Wasn't it absolutely marvelous, Samantha? Everyone will want Dominic to design for them now. Actually I think a lot of people have invited themselves back for drinks with just that in mind."

Samantha's heart sank. The last thing she felt like was a party, particularly if Jonathan was going to be there, but there was no way she could escape. She was an integral part of Dominic Blair so her presence would be expected.

She forced a smile. "I won't be long. I just need Dominic to help me get these dresses aboard, and then we'll join you."

Lilah laughed. "I don't think he is available for such a mundane activity right now. I swear he's wearing more lipstick than the models. Just look at his face."

Samantha looked and then turned away. Dominic's cheeks were streaked with lipstick where models and celebrities had kissed him. His eyes were sparkling. He was enjoying every moment of his popularity, reveling in the attention the fashion show had brought him. Maybe he had decided that success was more important than Sally, after all.

"I'll ask Jon to help you." Lilah scanned the crowd. "He's finished taking photographs so he can manhandle the dresses into the van and drive you home. Dominic can take the car you drove here when he's ready."

"No." Samantha's refusal was instantaneous but Lilah wasn't listening. Instead, she was already weaving her way through the crowd to where Jonathan was standing. As Samantha watched, frozen with horror, she saw him nod and begin to walk across the room.

Hurriedly, she turned to Myrna. "Would you help Jonathan bring out the dresses while I back the van up to the rear door?"

Without waiting for an answer, she crossed the floor to where Dominic was still surrounded by a chattering crowd. He handed her the keys to the van with a brief nod when she explained her intention, and then turned away, showing no further interest.

She slipped out of the back door and climbed into the van with a sob of despair while Jonathan and Myrna maneuvered the laden rails carefully across the restaurant. It was too much to ask of her. She still had to bear Jonathan's company for another four days while he first photographed the models in front of the hills behind the Hollywood Bowl, and then took individual shots of Lilah and her friends. How was she going to cope?

She turned the ignition fiercely and stabbed her foot down on the accelerator, jerking the gearstick into reverse. The van shot backwards too fast, narrowly missing a parked car, and screeched to a halt just as Jonathan propped open the double doors at the back of the restaurant.

He looked up with a frown, startled by the van's speed and the fact it had stopped about a foot away from him.

"You want to watch where you're going." His voice was sharp as Samantha switched off the engine. "You almost knocked me down."

When she didn't answer, he walked round to the driver's door, an expression of irritation on his face.

Samantha glared down at him from the driving seat. "How was I to know you were going to come charging through those doors just as I backed up? There was nobody there when I unlocked the van."

"Maybe you should have looked a bit more carefully." His voice was mild as he opened the door and put up his hand to help her down. "I didn't realize it was you behind the wheel."

"Would it have made any difference if you had?" Samantha ignored his hand and jumped to the ground.

It was a very silly thing for her to attempt, however, because her ankle was still weak and she was wearing open sandals with high heels. She gave a sharp gasp as she landed and clutched hold of the door.

"Are you all right?" Jonathan took a step forward and slipped his arm round her waist, taking her weight.

"Perfectly." After a fraction of a moment Samantha disengaged his arm and, ignoring the throb in her ankle and the sudden rapid beating of her heart, walked round to the back of the van to unlock the door.

He followed her and stood leaning against the side of the van as she fitted the key into the lock. He didn't say anything but just watched with interest while she jiggled it furiously. By her fifth attempt she was becoming flustered. Something was wrong with the lock. The door remained well and truly fastened while Jonathan continued to stand silently beside her, an interested audience of one.

Finally, she could bear it no longer. Her ankle ached, she was hot and tired, and any minute now he was going to ask her about her deception. As she had no intention of telling him the truth, she would have to think up a plausible explanation, one that didn't give away how she truly felt about him. She had to do something to stop him watching her with that amused expression too.

"See if you can do any better," she said, turning towards him with the keys in her hand. He was ahead of her, and before she finished speaking he had taken hold of both her hands and the keys.

"Insert them into the lock again." He pushed her arm downwards towards the van. "That's right. Now turn them slowly to the left, and push." He kept his hand tightly about her

161

fingers as he directed her, and with a click the van door swung open.

"It has a mind of its own," He said and then reached into the interior and released the bolt holding the other door in place.

"Thank you." Samantha tried to withdraw her hand, her voice stiff and unfriendly. "I shall know better next time."

"Will you really, Samantha?" His fingers tightened on hers, pressing them into the cold metal of the keys.

Angrily she swung towards him, but before she could speak he had backed her up against the van.

"Do you really learn from your mistakes, or are you so frightened of your emotions that you make the same ones over and over again?"

"Let me go." Samantha struggled against him, trying to free herself, nervous of the expression in his eyes, and the fact that they seemed to be alone. Most of the other cars had gone from the car park, and Myrna still hadn't appeared.

"Not until you tell me why you pretended to be involved with Dominic." Jonathan contained her struggles with contemptuous ease. "Why did you need that defense, Samantha? Were you afraid to face up to the attraction between us? Did it interfere with the even flow of your life? Perhaps you thought I'd go away if I thought Dominic was your lover and save you the messiness of having to deal with real human emotion. Why, Samantha? Why did you do it?"

"Because I was angry when you jumped to conclusions." Samantha stopped struggling and faced him, her face pale, her eyes full of scorn. "You stormed into my life without an invitation and made arrogant judgments, so I thought I'd teach you a lesson."

"Not good enough." Jonathan shook his head. "That explains your first deception in London, and I'll admit I deserved it, but why did you keep it up?"

"You wouldn't understand." Suddenly all the fight went out of her and she sagged against the van.

"Try me." His voice was unexpectedly gentle as he relaxed his hold on her arms.

For a brief moment she nearly gave way and explained everything, but then she remembered the scene between him and Sally outside her bedroom door only a few hours earlier. Shaking her head angrily and using the advantage of surprise, she twisted herself free.

With a muffled oath Jonathan reached out a long arm but she kicked at him with her stiletto heels and then backed away as he gave a yelp of pain.

"Keep your hands off me." Her voice shook with anger and fear. "My private life is nothing to do with you. Just once you persuaded me to act foolishly, but a lot has happened since then. Mind you, your Hollywood upbringing shows.

You even managed to delude Lilah into thinking you were serious about wanting a relationship with me. Perhaps you should abandon your photographic career and join your father behind a film camera. After all, you use the same techniques to get what you want. You think life is one big film set with every passing female ready and willing to be kissed into submission don't you?"

"Is that what you really think of me?"

"Yes, it is, and this time I'm not going to give you a chance to try and talk yourself out of it." Samantha's eyes were hard as she turned and hurried back into the restaurant to collect Myrna and the dresses.

Jonathan straightened up and watched her go, a twisted smile replacing the scowl on his face. Then he shook his head and followed her into the restaurant, looking anything but annoyed.

* * *

On the journey back to Lilah's house, Myrna did all the talking. She enthused about the dresses and the fashion show without pause for breath and apart from an occasional monosyllable, neither Samantha nor Jonathan interrupted her. They didn't look at one another either.

Samantha climbed down from the van as soon as it pulled into the driveway, and went in search of Dominic. He was out on the terrace, surrounded by the celebrities who were to model his designs for *Elite*. They were obviously discussing which dresses they preferred. At any other time Samantha would have been interested in their reactions, but now all she wanted to do was empty the van and then stay as far away from Jonathan as possible.

She touched her brother on the shoulder. "Dominic, will you go and help Jonathan carry the rails of dresses inside please. They're too heavy for me."

"Right away, Sam." Dominic removed his arm from Cheryl Napier's shoulder and pushed his way through the chattering women. "I won't be long, girls," he promised, winking at them.

She turned to them with a forced smile, remembering that they were her bread and butter, so she still had a job to do. Her smile froze as Cheryl Napier turned towards her, her glorious red hair glinting in the evening sun— because it wasn't Cheryl at all, but Sally. Sally had been nestling under Dominic's arm, the old Sally, alight with happiness, eyes sparkling and skin glowing.

She greeted Samantha with a giggle. "It worked, Sam. It really worked!"

"What did?"

"Ignoring Dominic, of course. Pretending I was interested in Jonathan." Sally threw her arms round Samantha and kissed her. "If I hadn't had such faith in your judgment, I could never have gone through with it. These last few days have been hell."

Suddenly she noticed the expression on Samantha's face and gave a shriek of laughter. "Don't tell me that I took you in, too, and after all that good advice you gave me. I thought you realized what I was up to, and that's why I kept away from you. I didn't want Dominic to think there was any collusion between us."

"You mean there's nothing between you and Jonathan?"

"Only friendship." Sally grinned. "He sometimes works with my brother, so I've often met him at dinner parties and social gatherings. In fact, to tell you the truth, I usually find him a bit stuffy, but the past few days have shown me another side of him."

"I bet they have," Samantha's voice was bitter. "He enjoys helping people make fools of themselves, doesn't he?"

"What's the matter?" Sally's eyes clouded with concern. "Surely you don't mind what I did to Dominic? After all, it was your idea."

"No, of course I don't and I'm really happy for you both." Samantha collected her thoughts as she gave Sally a hug. "But just tell me one thing. Exactly when did you and Dominic make up?"

"This morning." Sally gave another giggle. "He strode down to the terrace in a foul temper, lifted me out of the lounger where I was sunning myself, and dumped me in the pool. When I came up spluttering he had stripped off to his briefs and joined me. After that things just seemed to sort themselves out." She blushed faintly. "He asked me what I thought I was up to with Jonathan, and I accused him of having an affair with Lilah, and—well, we both burst out laughing because it was obvious, once he kissed me, that neither of us was remotely interested in anybody else."

"I suppose you told Jonathan straight away?" Samantha's face was pale.

"Yes, as a matter of fact I did. He seemed very surprised at first, but later he was more delighted than I would have thought possible. Then he did something surprising. He asked if we could keep up the pretense of our affair for a little longer."

"He did what?" Samantha's eyes began to burn with anger.

Sally shrugged. "It sounds stupid, doesn't it, but he said he had his reasons. Poor Dominic wondered what was happening when he saw us holding hands at Morton's, but at the first opportunity I explained everything and then, for some reason, he seemed to find it very funny. When he told Lilah, she burst out laughing, too. Look, here they come now." She broke off from her explanation and turned to where Dominic and Lilah were crossing the terrace.

"I've just been explaining everything," she began with a happy smile, but when she turned back, Samantha had gone.

It took Jonathan a long time to find Samantha, and when he did it was unexpected. He had searched the house, room by room, and pushed his way through the chattering guests, ignoring cries of recognition and friendly smiles. Finally, when he had begun to despair of ever finding her, he left the clamor of the terrace and the pool area and took the path behind the tennis court to the garden beyond.

She was sitting in the shadow of a rhododendron bush. Although she didn't move, the pale shimmer of her dress against the dark leaves gave her away. For a moment he hesitated and as he did so the floodlights came on, lighting up the pool area behind him and turning the water of the fountain into a myriad of colors.

Samantha looked up with a start and he swiftly melted back into the shadows as she left her seat and walked across the grass. When the changing lights bathed her face with color, highlighting the tearstains on her cheeks he gave a muttered oath, left the shelter of the overhanging bushes, and strode across the grass towards her.

She didn't see him coming until it was too late. As she backed away with a low cry, he stretched out an arm and clasped her loosely about the wrist.

"Say you forgive me." He pulled her towards him. "I only wanted to teach you a lesson, not make you look like this."

She tried to fight him, balling her hands into fists and pushing against him with all her strength, but it was an unequal struggle as Jonathan held her close, just waiting until she relaxed against him with a whimper of frustration.

"These last weeks have been hell," he continued, speaking as if she had already answered him. "From the moment I really looked at you in that French restaurant in Piccadilly, I knew I wanted you more than I've ever wanted anyone in my life. That's why I called at your office the following day before I went to the airport. I wanted to see you again so badly that it hurt. So when I found you in the bedroom with Dominic, it felt as if the bottom had fallen out of my world."

Something in the tone of his voice made Samantha stop fighting. She looked up at him, careless of the fresh tears that were washing her eyes.

"I was so angry when you jumped to conclusions about us," she finally answered him. "I just wanted to hurt you, do anything I could to deflate your ego."

"And you succeeded." He looked down at her, his face dark with the memory of their confrontation. "I traveled to Los Angeles under a cloud of bitterness and self-pity which only lifted slightly when Lilah told me you were arriving early and alone. When she asked me to meet you, and I saw you walking towards me across the airport terminal, I decided there and then that, Dominic or not, I was going to put up a fight. Stupidly I used the wrong approach. Because I thought you and Dominic were lovers, I assumed you were far more worldly wise in things of the heart than you really are, so I suggested an affair. It was arrogant but because I knew you were attracted to me, I persuaded myself that once we made love you wouldn't want Dominic anymore."

A feeling of warmth suffused Samantha at his words and she lowered her eyes, thankful that the changing lights hid the sudden flush on her cheeks.

"At first I hated you." Jonathan had to bend his head to catch her words. "You were moody and arrogant, and I found your assumption that I was ready for a casual affair insulting. But afterwards…"

"Afterwards, when I thought you'd drowned in the bath, you changed your mind. If I'd stopped to listen you would have told me you were Dominic's sister then, wouldn't you?" He tilted her chin gently, a smile returning to his mouth. "I realize that now, but because Lilah was waiting for us, and because I was certain that any talking we had to do would be better done later, I wouldn't let you explain."

Samantha didn't have to ask him what he meant by "later". His eyes told her.

"I've learned my lesson, Samantha. This time we'll do the talking first."

The controlled passion in his voice and the pressure of his fingers against her bare skin made her feel dizzy.

Jonathan's eyes darkened against the spangling lights as he pulled her close, his lips brushing her hair.

"Don't look at me like that," he groaned. "Not until I've said everything there is to say."

She could feel the strong beat of his heart against her, hear the sharp indrawn breath as she moved against him, the hardness of his body as he crushed her to him. She was suddenly filled with a sense of peace. Jonathan's arrogance, his moodiness, had been a defense against his unhappiness. With her he would always be his true self, whatever face he showed to the rest of the world. The knowledge freed her and she tilted her head back.

"You haven't told me about Sally yet, or your sudden trip to New York."

"It all began with an early morning telephone call." He shook his head wearily. "You weren't to know, but I've spent the last few months in Africa photographing the awful plight of the thousands of refugees there. It depressed me unbearably and then, just as I was leaving, a good collegue was involved in what is laughingly called an accident. He was robbed,

171

severely beaten and left for dead. When we eventually got him out of the country he was only just alive.

"He's been hovering between life and death for weeks in a New York hospital, and that early morning call was to tell me that although he had finally regained consciousness, he was very confused. The doctors told his wife to get me there if she possibly could, so I could answer his questions and explain what had happened."

"And Sally?" Samantha's eyes were soft as she watched the colored shadows chasing across his face. The expression in his eyes told her more about the strain he had been under than his words, and she now understood the melancholy withdrawals and the moodiness.

"Sally is his sister-in-law." Jonathan gave a wry smile. "She went to New York earlier to give her sister some support but by the time I arrived, the strain was beginning to show. Jack had been very aggressive for the twenty-four hours prior to my arrival—apparently a normal reaction for someone recovering from brain damage, but his behavior badly upset Sally.

"Once I realized we were on the same assignment, I packed her off to the airport, promising I would stay with her sister for as long as I could. She felt very guilty about going, as if she was letting everybody down, which is why she was so emotional when I arrived."

"And you took her straight into your arms." Samantha pulled away from him with a mock

172

frown. "I'd been counting the hours since you went and I was ready, right then, to confess about my deception with Dominic."

"And I walked straight past you to Sally." Jonathan gave Samantha his lopsided grin and it had its usual effect. "How was I to know that you would welcome a reunion in front of Dominic? I still thought you were lovers. And, besides, I'd had a bad time with Jack and my emotions were very frayed. I was far too vulnerable to cope with you in public. I wanted you all to myself. Believe me, Samantha, I needed you right then like you can't imagine, but I didn't think you were available."

"And I was so sure you had just been flirting with me, after all." Samantha shook her head. "When you walked past me, I was heartbroken—somehow it felt worse than when Danny died because you had brought me back to life and then trampled all over my heart."

"Danny?" Jonathan's face darkened. Samantha laughed softly, filled with a sense of power as she saw the spark of jealousy in his eyes.

"Danny died a lifetime ago," she told him. "We were very young and it was a tragedy. In fact until you came along, it has colored the whole of my life. Danny's death was the reason I wouldn't commit myself to anyone. I was frightened, you see. When you accused me of not wanting to deal with real human emotions

173

this evening, you were dangerously close to the truth."

"And now?" Jonathan's face relaxed, the lines smoothing away until he looked ten years younger.

"Now I want to know why you were still pretending to be having an affair with Sally after she told you about Dominic?" Samantha tried to sound angry, her hands pressed against his chest, feeling the heavy beating of his heart beneath her fingers.

"I told you, I wanted to teach you a lesson." Jonathan's smile faded. "It seemed a good idea at the time because I was furious with you for having deceived me for so long, and I was angry with Dominic and Lilah too. When Sally told me how she really felt about Dominic, I suddenly realized what she had been up to ever since I arrived back from New York. Until then, it honestly hadn't occurred to me. I just thought she wanted to be with me because we had both shared the trauma of Jack's injury. I was dumbfounded when I realized exactly what had been happening.

"I had very mixed feelings, too, because I still thought you were involved with Dominic." He grinned. "It took Lilah to point out the truth to me, because once she knew Dominic and Sally were a pair, she knew her little charade was over and she told me the truth. I was livid at first, but when she explained her reasons I began to see the funny side of it, and persuaded her not to let on to you. Dominic agreed as well, although he didn't realize I was going to turn the tables on him and carry on pretending with Sally. His face was a picture when he saw us holding hands."

"You mean Dominic was in on it too?" Samantha shook her head angrily. "How could he do it to me?"

"Easily." Jonathan grinned. "He said you needed to be shocked into an emotional reaction, forced back into the mainstream of life. But I think he felt I'd gone a little too far at Morton's, and that's why he told everyone that you were his sister. He didn't have time for full explanations but he didn't want you to be the only one left in the dark. He wanted to put you on your guard. After that, well you know the rest."

"And then you kissed Sally outside my bedroom door." Samantha scowled. "If I'd realized then that you were setting me up…"

"You'd have what?" Suddenly Jonathan was tired of talking. He pulled her close so that her hands were trapped between them, and began to kiss her, starting with the tip of her nose and ending, some moments later, with her mouth.

It was like a homecoming as their lips touched and then held, and Samantha felt a blossoming deep inside her that spread as his arms encircled her. When they drew apart, there was no further need for words.

Instead, Jonathan put his arm around her shoulders and turned her towards the house. She went obediently, ready to face the party, Dominic and Lilah's teasing, anything that he required of her. But he didn't take the path to the pool area. Instead, he led her across the lawn to the garage, and unlocked the door of the Mercedes.

"We have a date," he murmured as she hesitated. "In Malibu, remember?"

"But what will Lilah and Dominic think?"

"They won't even miss us." Jonathan kissed the back of her neck as he opened the car door. "Besides, there are several more things I want to say, and this isn't the place."

* * *

When they reached Malibu, it was late and the stars pricked the evening sky like scattered diamonds.

They had barely spoken on the journey, each of them knowing that real conversation was yet to come.

Jonathan drove the Mercedes into a secluded driveway without any explanation and then opened the car door and stepped out into the darkness. When Samantha joined him, they stood side by side, listening to the regular rhythm of the surf crashing against the shore.

"That's how I feel about you." Jonathan's voice was soft as he scooped her up into his

176

arms and began to carry her towards a long, low beach house. "My heart surges and then stops every time I look at you. I love you, Samantha, completely and forever. I never thought I would say that to anyone. My upbringing made me cautious. I learned, very early, to hide my real feelings, not to get too involved."

"And I learned to be frightened of love." Samantha tightened her arms around his neck, her fingers straying to his thick hair, blowing in the breeze.

"And now?" Jonathan let her slide the length of his body as he reached above the lintel for a hidden key.

"Now, I've learned from my mistakes," Samantha answered his earlier accusation with a teasing laugh. Then a new moon showed her the tormented expression on his face as he looked down at her and she knew that he needed to hear her say she loved him. Knew that beneath the arrogance and the moment of cruelty that had made him use Sally as a kind of revenge for his unhappiness, was the six-year-old boy Lilah had described to her. A little boy hungry for love.

"I love you, Jonathan." Her eyes glittered with momentary tears as she said the words she had never expected to use again.

As his lips sought hers, the silver moon obligingly disappeared behind a tiny wisp of cloud. And when it finally found them again, by peeping in through a bedroom window, it painted chains of silver filigree across their bodies so that as they moved together, talking without words, learning about each other with every sigh and murmured endearment, it bound them together.

The End.

If you *loved* this book
(or even just liked it)

Please leave a review ...
Authors need reviews! Keep this author writing

Other Books We Love books by Sheila Claydon:

Cabin Fever
Reluctant Date
Double Fault
Kissing Maggie Silver
Mending Jodie's Heart (When Paths Meet Book 1)
Finding Bella Blue (When Paths Meet Book 2)
Saving Katy Gray (When Paths Meet Book 3)
Miss Locatelli
Remembering Rose (Mapleby Memories Book 1)
The Sheila Claydon Special Edition

BWL Author
Sheila Claydon

In the 1980s Sheila Claydon wrote a number of romances under the pseudonym Anne Beverley. Then a busy career and family life got in the way and before she knew it, she had turned her back on the characters who were begging to be liberated from her imagination. Now she is back to writing fiction again and, considerably older and no longer shy, writes under her own name.

Her motto is a quote by the late Ray Bradbury: "First, find out what your hero wants. Then just follow him."

Although family remains central to her life, she still finds the time to read, to write, and to travel. Many of the places she has visited feature in her books. Her fans say that reading them is like buying a ticket to romance.

You can find her at https://www.facebook.com/SheilaClaydon.author/

bookswelove.com

www.ingramcontent.com/pod-product-compliance
Lightning Source LLC
Chambersburg PA
CBHW051125260626
47170CB00005B/1667